Housebreaking
a Husband

Housebreaking
a Husband

Lori Soard

Five Star • Waterville, Maine

Five Star First Edition Romance Series.

Published in 2002 in conjunction with
Hyatt Literary Agency.

Set in 11 pt. Plantin by Myrna S. Raven.

Printed in the United States on permanent paper.

Library of Congress Cataloging-in-Publication Data

Soard, Lori.
    Housebreaking a husband / Lori Soard.
       p. cm.
    Five Star first edition romance series.
    ISBN 0-7862-4578-6 (hc : alk. paper)
    1. Dog trainers — Fiction. 2. Custody of children —
Fiction. 3. Twins — Fiction. 4. Domestic fiction.
5. Love stories.
PS3619.O37 H68 2002
    813'.6—dc21   2002026772

Dedication

To Fern Michaels who mentored me, supported me and has become a dear friend. May all your dreams come true. To Laura Cifelli, who believed in this story and helped me mold it. I learned a great deal from your input. To Russell Davis who loved the story enough to stay up late and read it. To the Success Sisters, you've been there from the first. Thanks for your support, friendship and fierce critiques.

Chapter One

Two sets of tomato red handprints spaghettied the walls, the washing machine spewed white foam, and purple crayon marks now took center stage on his once-white living room walls.

Turning his back on the mess, Trent Kasey answered the insistent peal of the doorbell. He stared blankly at the burly man in tattered overalls on his doorstep.

"Apollo Movers."

"You've got the wrong house." He heard Caitlin wail as Kyle buried his chubby toddler fingers in her hair and pulled.

The man held up his clipboard and tapped it with his forefinger. "Twenty-nine thirty-two Viewpoint."

"That's this address, but I didn't call you." He tried to grab Kyle with one hand to prevent him from snatching Caitlin bald.

"A Mr. Nathan Winters hired us to move the belongings of Caitlin and Kyle Winters."

A swift blaze of fury lit a fire in Trent's veins.

"Tell Mr. Winters that Caitlin and Kyle will be staying right here."

The man shrugged. "Whatever you say, buddy. I don't care as long as I get my money."

The man scribbled a few notes on his clipboard before climbing into his truck and rumbling away. Slamming the door, Trent jabbed the speed dial number for his lawyer.

"Kyle, stop poking your sister like that." He cradled the phone against his ear as he tried to keep his twenty-two-month-old twin niece and nephew under control while he explained the situation to his lawyer.

"Calm down, Trent. Everything's fine." Gregg's voice dribbled soothing words.

"Just tell me there's no way a judge would give the kids to that man. He's a swindler, for God's sake. He hasn't been there for the twins or Melissa. The kids don't even know him!"

He grabbed Caitlin with one arm and settled her on his hip. He pressed a gentle kiss into her baby-shampooed hair. A fist tightened around his heart. God, how he loved these kids.

"I wish I could give you better news, Trent. But the courts favor natural parents. He's married, so the father offers a more stable home environment. At least on the surface."

"The man's a crook—"

Gregg Roberts cut him off. "It doesn't matter. We would have to prove that, and we can't. Of course, if you had a more stable home life, your chances would be a little better. You work all hours, and single parenting is tough."

"Stable how? Anything. I'll do anything."

"Say if you were married."

Married? He grimaced. Marriage was something he'd avoided. Once, he'd asked a woman to marry him. That hadn't worked out. Since then, he'd never felt the urge to commit himself to one woman for a lifetime.

"Don't hold your breath." Especially since he wasn't even dating anyone at the moment.

"There isn't anyone special? Now might be a great time to elope to Vegas." Gregg chuckled.

There was no one special. The women he'd dated in the past would never marry an instant family. Nor would he trust them to be the kind of mother Caitlin and Kyle needed.

"Kyle blah blah," Caitlin insisted. He only understood the word "Kyle."

"What are my other options?" There was no sign of his nephew in the room. No telling what he was getting into. Time to end this conversation quickly. Otherwise, he'd be repainting the living room walls to hide fresh crayon marks.

"That *is* your option, buddy. Elope to Vegas or kiss those kids good-bye. Crook or not, involved in the past or not, courts will award custody to the father."

"Kyle blah blah." Caitlin pointed toward the kitchen.

"That's no option, Gregg. I'll see you Friday for the hearing." He dropped the phone back in the cradle, set Caitlin down, and went in search of Kyle. The boy tended to wander off but he couldn't yet open doors.

Trent's jaw dropped. The back door stood open wide.

The deserted beach lay cast in shadows as the sun fell into the indigo waters of the Pacific. Sarah's gaze followed the flight of a few lone seagulls as they circled above her for some scrap she might be kind enough to throw out.

Nightfire tugged on his lead, refusing to heel. As a dog trainer, Sarah knew her animals should be better behaved. But Night still had a lot of puppy in him despite his large size. It was a good thing she'd made a fortune off her dog-training kit because if any potential clients got a glimpse of Night, her career would be over.

A small boy sat on a log near the edge of the water. She frowned. He seemed much too young to be out by himself.

"Mind if I sit down?" she asked.

"Want Umcil Twempt."

She had no idea what the child had just said. He scooted

closer to her and crawled onto her lap; his tiny thumb sought the safety of his mouth.

The heat from his little body filled her heart. A fierce ache burned through Sarah's gut. God, how she wanted a child. Her arms would feel empty later without a child of her own to hold. It was never to be. Children were not in her future.

"Where do you live?" The sooner she returned the little guy to his parents, the sooner she could get back to her life. The one without children. The one with dogs for company. Dogs were fine company.

The little boy jabbered nonsense and pointed up the beach. She rose and started walking.

"Let's just walk this way. I'll bet someone is frantic over you. What's your name?" she asked him.

"Kwyle."

She frowned. Poor kid. He was trying to talk to her and she couldn't understand a word he was saying. Surely his name wasn't Kwa? Perhaps she should just pretend to understand what he said?

"My name is Sarah."

" 'Arah."

"Very good." Not bad, considering it was the first word he'd uttered that made sense.

She stopped walking as they neared the end of the row of houses nestled along the ridge overlooking the beach. Surely the child couldn't have wandered this far away from his home?

"Which is your house?"

The little boy ignored her and made a move toward Nightfire.

"Doggie."

Nightfire cowered away, apparently unsure of what this

strange miniature creature intended.

"His name is Nightfire. You can pet him."

Nightfire whimpered and began to shiver.

"Oh, you silly dog. There is nothing to be scared of."

Kwa touched the end of Night's nose, and the dog yelped and sprinted away before Sarah could grab his leash. She grabbed the boy in her arms and took off after the dog.

"Dumb mutt," she muttered, even though Night was a purebred black Labrador, a normally intelligent breed.

Her fingertips brushed the tip of Nightfire's collar. A man's shout startled her and the dog sprinted out of her reach. The man ran toward them. Sarah's mouth lost all moisture as she noted the man's height.

Night stopped. Looked at the man. Looked back at Sarah. Looked at the little boy. Gave another yelp and ran in circles around the approaching man.

Now closer, Sarah saw that the man carried a small child with him. The little girl was a replica of the boy, only with a head full of glossy black hair. She was perched on the man's shoulders.

"Kyle. Kyle. Thank God." His gentle face creased with worry.

She relaxed. The man wasn't a maniac; he was frantic with worry that his son was missing.

Nightfire continued to run in circles, winding his leash tightly about the man's ankles.

"Night, halt," she shouted, but her command was lost on the still-terrified dog.

She made a frantic lunge for him, but the dog was too fast, and the leash, now too short, trapped the man.

In a tangle of arms, four furry legs, and sand, they collided. Just before the man fell, Sarah grabbed the toddler atop his shoulders.

11

★ ★ ★ ★ ★

Trent lay flat on his back staring up at an angel. She held Caitlin in her arms, and Kyle clung to her leg with wide eyes. His chest hurt as he drew in his first gasp of air since the fall.

"I'm so sorry." Her wide blue eyes were filled with humor.

"Twent boo boo?" Caitlin's lips trembled.

Since their mother's death, both children were sensitive to anyone being hurt or ill. They'd seen their mom get sicker and sicker before she died. Trent shuddered as he remembered the cancer ravaging her body. He forced another breath into his lungs, intent on reassuring them. It burned a fiery path down his throat.

The woman was still hovering, her thick cloud of tawny hair curled over her shoulders and wrapped protectively around Caitlin. She held her free hand down to him, and he grasped it and allowed her to help him up. He hid his embarrassment by swiping the sand off the back of his legs.

If he *had* to fall, why couldn't it have been because he was tangled up with those gorgeous legs of hers instead of in her dog's leash?

Chapter Two

She tried not to notice how green the man's eyes were. They weren't the color of moss on the shady side of a tree, and even if they were, she didn't notice. Nor did she notice the way his shirt pulled tight across muscular shoulders. Besides, he was obviously married with a family.

"Are you okay?" she asked, ignoring the way one strand of dark hair trailed onto his forehead, making her fingers itch to smooth it back. She really needed to get this mothering instinct under control. Except her thoughts toward this man were anything but motherly.

"Fine." His voice rumbled like water over smooth rocks. He held out his hand. "Trent Kasey."

"Sarah Goldwyne."

She placed her hand in his. *Married,* she reminded herself, as the heat of his touch traveled up her arm. She took a deep breath. He didn't really have dimples like Clark Gable. And even if he did, it wasn't her place to notice them, it was his wife's.

Trent Kasey took a step toward the little boy still clinging to her legs, winced and limped the next step.

"You're hurt," she cried. She dropped to her knees and looked closer at his ankle.

"I'll be fine."

She looked up at him and noticed that his face paled, and his dimples turned to grooved lines in his cheeks. Stubborn man, but typical. With three brothers, she should be used to men trying to be macho instead of admitting that they might need a little help. Used to it or not, she'd never been one to stroke a man's ego.

"It looks like it's sprained." She ran her hands lightly over the already-swelling ankle. "How far is your house?"

Trent nodded to the south. "Twenty-nine thirty-two."

"Twenty-nine thirty-two?" she croaked. The house next door to the one she'd just rented. She wasn't even finished moving in. Just great. Not only was her treacherous body attracted to a man who was married, but fate decided to flaunt his happy family life almost within touching distance. As though thumbing its nose at her that she could never have what she wanted.

"It's not far. I can make it, if you'll just—"

"You'll need help with the children." There. That should soothe his ruffled ego enough for him to allow her to help.

"Thanks. I'm still trying to get this parenting thing perfected."

She frowned. Were they his stepchildren? Or perhaps he wasn't involved with the children. The image of the little girl clinging to his neck and looking at him with trusting eyes told her that he was a loving father.

"How old are your children?"

"They aren't my children. They're my niece and nephew. Twenty-two months."

Not his children? Her eyes sought his left hand in the increasingly dim twilight. Impossible to tell if he wore a ring. Why did she care anyway? She had nothing to offer a man like him. He obviously loved children, and she couldn't give him that.

"Do you have the kids over often?" She grabbed his arm, placed it around her shoulders, and slid her other arm around his waist.

He didn't comment, which told Sarah more than his pronounced limp that he needed her help. *God but he smells good.* Like pine needles and crisp wood. Like a rumbling fire in the fireplace. Like every memory she'd ever wanted to hold on to and every tradition she never could.

"Kyle. Caitlin. Follow Uncle Trent."

The small children clasped hands and followed along behind them. She couldn't help but smile. They looked like sweet little cherubs, but she knew appearances could be deceiving. She'd bet those two could get into more trouble than she and all her brothers combined had ever thought of.

"How did Kyle get away from you?" she asked.

"He has a tendency to wander off, but I didn't think he could open doors. Guess he learned a new trick this week."

She chuckled. "Ever hear of locking a door? You should be able to find the attachments at any store."

Her entire side was on fire where it brushed against his as they walked. She took a deep breath. She was just lonely. That was all. After three years without a man's touch, she would have reacted the same to any man.

"They make those? We've never had to use them in Soul's Harbor, but I guess I'll have to start."

Sarah laughed. She loved a man with a sense of humor. Did he have to be just what she'd always wanted in a mate? She still didn't know if he was married. Besides, she couldn't get in a relationship. She was just starting to build her business. She didn't have *time* for a man.

"Will your wife be worried?" she asked.

"No. Will your husband?"

She felt the heat creep into her cheeks and was thankful for the crisp night air that cooled her flush and hid its deep red from the man next to her. He knew she'd been fishing.

"I'm not married. I almost got married once, but it

didn't work out. I'd rather be alone than deal with that heartache again."

"I'm not married either."

She breathed a sigh of relief but wasn't sure why. She didn't want a relationship. Did she? She shook her head.

"Almost there."

His only response was a grunt. His ankle must hurt because his limp grew worse. The steps up from the beach were difficult to navigate. She compared the children's short legs to the empty space between each step. How were they going to manage getting to the top in one piece? He grasped the railing and pulled himself up the twenty-five steps, while Sarah got behind the kids and steadied their backs.

A fine sheen of perspiration shone on her forehead by the time she was finished. The overhead light glowed with soft yellow phosphorescence and showed that Trent's face had turned a pasty white.

"Are you okay?" She touched his arm.

He waved her away. "Fine." But he was breathing heavily.

"I think you should have a doctor look at that ankle."

"I'm fine." He turned to walk toward his house and stumbled.

She rushed to his side and wrapped an arm around his waist. "Stubborn man."

"Nagging woman." But his tone was light, and he accepted her help.

"Kyle. Caitlin. Follow us please." Much to Sarah's surprise, the children obeyed her. Good thing, because she didn't know how she could have gotten them all home any other way.

He'd left his door unlocked, as most of the residents of

Soul's Harbor did. She pushed it open and helped him to the couch, where he sank down with a sigh.

The living room was littered with toys of all shapes and sizes. She raised her brows.

"You certainly keep a lot of toys around."

"Kyle and Caitlin live with me."

Close your mouth before you catch flies, dear. Her mother's voice sang through her head. It sounded so much like her mother that Sarah glanced over her shoulder to make sure she wasn't in the room.

"Guess that's that," he muttered.

"That's what?" Sarah leaned over and flipped on the TV, tuning in to a kids' show to distract the busy twins.

Both children plopped onto the floor and gazed in awe at the screen.

"How did you do that?"

She shrugged. "I have young cousins. Kids like certain shows. I just got lucky and found one. You didn't answer my question. That's what?"

He sighed. "This is the point where you make a flimsy excuse and leave."

Well, now that he mentioned it . . . What was the point in staying? She'd helped him home, done all she could. They were neighbors, and she'd done her neighborly duty. She'd lost one child and been told she couldn't have more. If Paul, her fiancé, hadn't been able to handle that news, how could she expect anyone else to accept it? No, she was better off not getting involved. She would only be hurt again.

"Have the kids eaten?" Now why had she asked that?

"Spaghetti. The evidence is still on the kitchen walls."

There was really no other reason for her to stay. "In that case, I'll be going." She turned toward the door, a sense of unknown loss weighing so heavily on her she could barely move.

"Sarah?"

His voice stopped her just as she placed her hand on the cool metal doorknob.

"I think I do need that doctor."

She spun around. His face was pinched in pain, and his ankle had swelled to the size of a tennis ball. Rushing back to his side, she stared at his ankle and wondered how she was going to fit two children, a large man, and herself into an Explorer packed with boxes, and dog crates.

"I think it's broken." His breathing was heavy.

"Broken? You walked home on a broken ankle?" She stood and placed her hands on her hips. Of all the stupid, childish, macho things to do . . .

"How else was I going to get home?" His lips quirked the tiniest bit.

"I'll drive."

"I'm sorry, Sarah. If it weren't for Kyle and Caitlin, I'd handle it on my own. But, there just isn't anyone else who can help with them in an emergency."

She swallowed. So she was the lucky candidate. She got to experience the joy of being around children for a few short hours and then go home to an empty, lonely house that would never know the laughter of a child.

"No problem," she said. But it was a problem, and after today she didn't plan ever to see Trent Kasey or his niece and nephew again.

Dancing on hot coals with Satan would have felt better than the throb in his ankle. Trent rested his head against the back of the passenger seat and tried not to groan. Kyle and Caitlin grew uncharacteristically quiet in the backseat.

He wondered if they remembered their mother being taken to the hospital, the chemotherapy, how sick she'd been. The poor kids were probably terrified he'd meet the same fate and they'd never see him again. Pushing down the swift stab that inched up his calf, he turned and glanced over his shoulder at them.

One tiny thumb found its way into Kyle's mouth, and Caitlin clutched a tattered blanket. Both sets of eyes were wide and terrified.

"Hey, guys. It's just a little boo-boo on Uncle Trent's ankle." He reached back and ruffled each dark head of hair, the effort causing more pain.

Caitlin blew him a kiss. He smiled.

"Everything is going to be just fine." He wasn't sure if he said the words to reassure himself or the children.

Sarah shifted into gear with a grinding of metal that set his teeth on edge. His Camaro was undergoing abuse that he never would have inflicted on it. Not that it mattered. The car was going to have to go anyway. It just wasn't practical with two small children. He'd have to trade it for a minivan. The thought made him squirm in his seat a little. A minivan seemed so domesticated.

"Sorry," Sarah muttered. "You would have had more room to spread out in my Explorer, but it's jammed full of boxes of dog treats and crates." He forced himself to shrug. "I'm selling it anyway."

"You're kidding? You're going to sell this cherry?"

He laughed. "It's not very practical for a man with two small children."

She grew quiet. Something he noticed she did each time he mentioned family or children. He frowned. She was a total stranger. There was no reason he should get the feeling that she really did like children. Her reaction was

19

that of a dozen women he'd dated. The minute they discovered he had a family, they lost interest. Well, he'd just stay single. He and Caitlin and Kyle were a team. A complete package. If a woman chose to love one of them, she chose to love them all.

"I want to buy it." Squealing into third gear, she let off on the clutch a second too soon.

The rebound was like a kick in the seat of the pants and sent fresh shards of pain through his ankle. He gritted his teeth.

"I don't think so."

She narrowed her eyes. "Why not? I don't have a family."

Her lips turned down the tiniest bit at the corners. No, she didn't have a family and, if her expression was anything to go by, the thought made her very sad.

The car was too powerful for her. Too fast. Too sporty. Not her style. So, why had she offered to buy it? Because he'd said it wasn't a family car. It had been a moment of rebellion against fate. Why should she drive a practical Ford Explorer when her only family consisted of a dog? She might as well enjoy life. Let loose.

"How did Caitlin and Kyle come to live with you?" She shifted down as she slowed for a stop, and the car jerked a little from her inexperienced handling.

Right, like she had any business owning a car like this. Something twisted painfully in her chest. She didn't belong in a family but didn't fit the single lifestyle either. So, what did that leave? Some kind of in-between limbo?

"My sister died three months ago."

"What happened to her?"

"Melissa died of cancer." His voice fell flat.

"I'm so sorry." She laid a hand on his arm and heard him draw in a quick breath. It was a small comfort, realizing that he was attracted to her, too. Shame it could never go further than that.

Chapter Three

It was the day Sarah dreaded all week and looked forward to at the same time.

"Sarah, we wondered if you'd make it this time." Her mother hugged her tightly, the scent of fresh-squeezed lemonade filled the air.

"I only missed one week, Mom. Matt and Jeff miss all the time."

"Yes, but you're our baby." Her mother sniffed.

She gazed up at the ceiling, praying for either patience or divine intervention.

"Not that I'd mind you missing our traditional Sunday dinner if it was for a man." Catherine Goldwyne stirred a big pitcher of lemonade with a long wooden spoon.

"No chance of that." She dipped her finger in a bowl of chocolate frosting and brought the creamy concoction to her mouth. She closed her eyes. "Heaven. You make the best chocolate cake, Mom."

"Quit changing the subject." Catherine crossed her arms tightly across her chest and tapped her shoe on the Spanish tiles.

"We've had this discussion before." She picked up the icing spatula and dropped a glob of chocolate frosting onto the cooled cake on the counter.

"Any man would be lucky to have you." Catherine stirred the lemonade hard enough to splash tiny yellow droplets onto the counter.

"Picking on Sarah again, Mom?" Matt, Sarah's oldest brother, crossed the room and planted a kiss on Catherine's

★ ★ ★ ★ ★

Two hours later, the leftovers were stored away, and the kitchen sparkled and smelled of ammonia. She stood in the doorway of the living room, watching her father. He leaned forward in his recliner, intent on the game playing out on the TV. His once-thick brown hair held one balding spot in the very center of his head.

"You idiot! Catch the ball."

"I'm gonna take off, Daddy." She moved to his chair and sat on the arm, just as she'd done for all twenty-six years of her life.

"Why so sad, munchkin?" Her father looked up at her.

She shrugged. "No reason."

"You can't let your mother get to you. She means well." His gaze strayed to the television for a moment. "Oh, man! I can't believe he missed that."

"Daddy?"

"Hmmm?"

"You and Mom do understand that I—that I—" Sarah swallowed. "That I won't be having any children?"

"Oh, sweetheart, we know what the doctors said. We just aren't sure they were right. Your mother loves you. She wants the best for you."

She felt a flash of irritation. "Just like she wanted what was *best* for my baby?" It seemed her entire life, her mother had wanted the best for her. The best had included no sleepovers with her girlfriends, no dating until she was seventeen, and wearing a hopelessly out-of-date brides-maid-style dress to her senior prom because it was *proper*. And when she was twenty-two, unwed, and pregnant, her mother had tried to convince her to give her child up for adoption. Did her mother want what was best for her or just to control her?

"Sweetheart, don't let your mother worry you. No one was going to make you give that baby up for adoption, regardless of what that bastard Paul did to you. It was our grandchild."

"Thanks, Daddy. I feel like I'm being judged sometimes." Sarah sighed.

"Paul was dragging his heels about marrying you, and I was glad—I didn't think you should marry him. Who cares if he was the baby's father? He was a jerk, and he didn't deserve you. We're family, and we stick together."

Sarah felt the tears coming. She sniffed. "Paul didn't love me."

"I could kill Paul for what he did to you, but don't let it keep you down, Sarah. Not all men are jerks like Paul—look around you, this family is full of steady, honest men."

Sarah hugged her father tightly. "You're so right. And I love all of you to pieces. I guess I'd better go. I'll try to make it next week."

"Okay." Her father turned back to the game.

She watched him for a moment, wanting to say more but not sure where she would even start.

"Hello, Legs." He whistled.

Sarah perched on a ladder; cutoff shorts showed her legs to best advantage. He held back a groan. Did his next-door neighbor have to be quite so appealing? He wasn't prepared for a serious relationship, and he had a feeling a woman like Sarah Goldwyne would settle for nothing less.

"Need some help?" Now why had he said that? The farther he stayed away from her, the better. He didn't want to get involved. Caring only hurt. Hadn't life confirmed that more than once?

"No, thanks. You're an invalid at the moment, until that

26

Ace bandage comes off anyway. Besides, I can handle it."

She probably could. Every time she'd been around him, she'd been more than eager to get away. Why did that irritate him? He should be thankful. No attachments.

"Where are the twins?"

"Napping. They take a two-hour nap every day. It's my only break."

She chuckled. "They do seem like a handful. How are you going to manage juggling twins and work?"

"I own a construction company, but my head foreman has been handling things the past few months. I'm interviewing nannies this week. I have to get back, or the business will suffer."

She stretched to hang the second basket of vivid pink petunias from her front porch. As she stood on tiptoe, her already short cutoffs moved up another half inch. His mouth went dry. He'd been joking when he'd called her "Legs," but her legs were the longest he'd ever seen. They seemed to go on forever. He allowed his gaze to roam up the length of them again.

"Enjoying the view?" Sarah asked.

His gaze shot up to hers. She grinned, and he flushed. Barely biting back a curse, he forced himself to focus on her face. Not that it cooled him off any. She was gorgeous.

"Do you know anyone in the area who might be a good nanny?" he asked.

She tilted her head to the side. "Not really. Most of the local women either work or are socialites who wouldn't want to take on baby-sitting."

"That's what I was afraid of."

"Did you check the newspaper?"

"I'm terrified to leave them with a stranger." He ran his hands through his hair. What if someone was mean to

Caitlin and Kyle? Or what if they didn't watch Kyle closely enough, and he got hurt?

"I would be too. Maybe a nanny service could help."

"Still interested in my Camaro?" Every nerve in his body screamed out against selling it. He leaned against his crutches.

She looked down at him for a moment, a knowing grin on her face. "You don't really want to sell it, do you?"

"Not really." He didn't see the sense in keeping it, though. He had to have something bigger.

"I was thinking. What if we made a trade?"

"Trade?" His Camaro for her Explorer? Somehow that didn't seem like a fair trade to Trent. The Explorer was worth far more than his car.

"Sure. I get to drive your Camaro on the weekends for fun and when I don't need it for clients. You get to drive my Explorer when you need it to haul the kids around. We both get the best of both worlds."

He thought for a moment. Not to mention he'd get to see Sarah every time they traded cars. He grinned. If he could stand the sound of her grinding gears every time she pulled out of the driveway, it just might work.

"Let's give it a try."

"Great. This weekend?" She hooked the last hanging basket onto a plant hook and started down the ladder.

"Sure. Let me steady the ladder for you." He dropped the crutches and grabbed both sides of the ladder as Sarah descended.

Big mistake. First her ankles came into view, then the length of her long, sexy legs. He closed his eyes. She was close enough that he could feel her warmth. One of her legs brushed against him as she stepped off the ladder and turned to face him.

"Thanks." Her voice rasped over his nerve endings.

He opened his eyes. Too close. His arms still held the ladder, creating a circle she stood within. If he lowered his head just a fraction, those soft full lips would meet his. What would she taste like?

"I—uh—I have to get back and check on the twins." He stuttered again. What was it about this woman that changed him into a blithering idiot? He leaned down to retrieve his crutches. His sprain should be healed within a few days, and then he could get rid of the cumbersome things.

"See ya later." She grabbed another basket of brilliant pink flowers and started back up the ladder.

He didn't like her on that ladder by herself. What if she got hurt?

"Sure you don't need some help?"

"I'm fine, Trent. Go watch Kyle so he doesn't get into any trouble. I certainly don't need anyone else in my life babying me."

He frowned. Seemed he'd been dismissed. Just as well. Another minute looking at those long legs, and he would have been a goner.

"Is it okay to have my boyfriend over?" The potential nanny popped her gum loudly.

He took a deep breath.

"Thank you for driving out, Ms. Nichols. I'll be making a decision later in the week."

"Did I get the job?" the girl asked eagerly.

He stared at her tongue ring as she spoke. He couldn't help it. Every time she opened her mouth, the silver flashed. Didn't that hurt?

"Actually, I think I'm looking for someone a bit—older." Older and more stable.

"Oh, shoot. I really wanted to work for you. You're so cute." The girl pinched his cheek. "Oh, well. If you ever need a date, big guy, you have my number."

Unbelievable. He'd interviewed twelve possible nannies so far, and each had been worse than the one before. Not a single one he would have trusted with the care of Caitlin and Kyle. What was he going to do? He had a meeting tomorrow with one of the biggest developers in Soul's Harbor. He needed the work.

It was 2:10. Nanny number thirteen would be arriving any minute. Loud rock music rattled the windows of his house. He pulled the curtain back and peeked at nanny thirteen. No way in this world.

When the doorbell rang, Trent opened it to a young man in leather jacket and chains. "I'm sorry to waste your time. The position has been filled."

"Oh, man!" The wanna-be biker kicked at the front step and stomped back to his car.

Trent shut the door behind him and leaned his forehead against it. He was a drowning man, and the tropical storm had just been upgraded to a hurricane.

Sarah watched the parade of nanny candidates grow steadily worse. "Night, surely Trent wouldn't be insane enough to leave the kids with one of those wackos?"

Night whined. His tail thumped against the soft grass.

"I agree, boy. But it's none of our business."

She threw a red ball across the yard. Night bounded after it, caught it, and promptly lay down on his belly.

"Bring it back, Night. Here boy. Come on. Fetch means you go get it *and* bring it back."

"Do you think he understands you?" Trent stood on the other side of the hedge.

"Some of it, anyway." She shrugged. She always talked to her animals. So what if others thought she was insane? "How's the nanny hunt going?"

"Terrible. Everyone from a biker to a Valley girl has applied."

She laughed. "I saw. What are you going to do?"

"I don't know. Actually, I was coming over to ask you for a favor."

Uh-oh. She felt her entire body stiffen. If he was going to ask her to baby-sit the twins, she just couldn't. Every day would be a reminder of what she could never have. To top it off, when Trent came home she would be forced to come back to an empty house. Each day might be a dream, but each night would be a misery.

"I have an extremely important meeting tomorrow. It could make or break my business." Trent's mossy green eyes pleaded with her.

She shifted uncomfortably. If only his eyes weren't the color of moss.

"Could you watch them for just a couple of hours? I know it's a terrible imposition. I'd pay you."

Would one day really hurt? Yes, but the image of the sub-par nanny candidate in chains blared loud and clear.

"That's not necessary. I'd be happy to watch them."

She must be a glutton for punishment. But she couldn't bear the thought of an escaped lunatic from a mental institution, serial killer, or bitter, hateful woman watching out for the twins. And it was only for one day . . .

Trent grabbed her hand and brought her knuckles up to his lips. "Thank you, Sarah. I need to leave at noon."

He spun awkwardly on one foot and hobbled with crutches back into his house. When the door closed behind him, Sarah brought her hand up to her cheek.

"Stop acting like a schoolgirl, you ninny." She brought her hand back down to her side. A hand that still tingled from where he'd pressed his lips to it.

At 11:45, Sarah crossed the short distance between her yard and Trent's and knocked on the front door. It swung open quickly, throwing her off-balance.

"Sarah, thank God."

"Nice to see you, too." She couldn't help laughing at the scattered toys littering the living room floor and the stain Trent tried to scrub off his tie.

The strong aroma of peanuts surrounded him. "Peanut butter?" she asked.

"Kyle and Caitlin can't seem to eat without getting food on the walls, me, or both."

"It may have something to do with what you feed them. Spaghetti, peanut butter . . ."

"Good point. There's just one problem."

She couldn't focus on his words because it was hard to ignore that slow sexy smile of his and concentrate at the same time.

"Hmmm?"

"I only know how to fix two things. Spaghetti and peanut butter and jelly."

She laughed. "Do you have another tie?"

"One."

"Then go change and get going before you're late for your meeting. The twins will be fine."

But she wouldn't be if he kept snatching tiny pieces of her heart.

Chapter Four

"Hey, kiddos, want to plant some flowers around Sarah's house?"

Kyle clapped his hands.

"I'll take that as a yes. Let's go." She took two tiny hands and led them outside.

Grabbing some brightly colored petunias she'd started from seeds, Sarah handed each twin two plants and juggled six herself.

"When I was little, my mother would let me help her in the garden," she told them.

"Momma?" Kyle asked.

"Yes, sweetie. We would spend hours talking and planting. There's something very elemental about digging your hands into the earth."

Kyle sank both hands into the moist soil of the flower bed she had weeded and tilled last week and grinned up at her. Sarah's heart twisted.

"That's it, buddy."

Grasping two fistfuls of dirt, he lifted his hands and promptly buried them in his sister's hair. Caitlin wailed.

She patted her on the back. "It's just a little dirt. It'll wash off." She handed Caitlin a flower. "Kyle, tell your sister you're sorry. Now, you two help Sarah plant this."

Caitlin knelt down and gently placed the flower in the small hole Sarah had dug with her gardening spade.

"Perfect, Caitlin. Now we fill in the hole and we have a flower."

"Want f'owers there." Kyle pointed to his front porch.

Sarah patted him on the top of his head. "Great idea, buddy. I have some small pots with petunias. Let's set them on your porch and down the walkway." Sarah handed each child two small plastic pots with bright pink, purple, and white petunias, and they arranged them on the front stoop. Two more trips to Sarah's house for more petunias, and they were finished.

"Look how pretty." She stood back and surveyed their gardening. The house suddenly looked lived in. As though a family had put roots there.

A lump lodged in her throat. Family. Something she'd always had in a sense, but something she also yearned for. Just as she'd feared, being with the twins had made that ache more poignant. Perhaps bringing Kyle and Caitlin into her life was God's way of giving her a tiny piece of what she could never have. Maybe she should rethink baby-sitting full-time.

Complete and total disaster. That was the only way Trent could think to describe his meeting with Rick Matthews. The man stressed he wanted someone reliable. Someone who could deliver deadlines and quality. Someone who could find a parking spot that wasn't three miles away and who could walk rather than hobble into the restaurant fifteen minutes late. Not that the man had been vicious enough to comment on his halting progress. Instead he had pinpointed weaknesses that Trent couldn't deny or blame on a temporary sprain.

Trent flipped the radio on, then back off.

"I understand from your foreman that you haven't been around much the last few months." Rick had stared at him with an unblinking gaze.

He squirmed in the seat of his Camaro. He couldn't

deny Rick's comments. He hadn't been around much. Maybe he should have pleaded for mercy. Told Rick Matthews how hard it was to juggle twins and work. Explained that he planned to hire a nanny. Let Rick know that his ankle should be healed within a few days, and he'd be more mobile.

"It's amazing I got the job." He refused to explain himself to anyone. The twins came first. Period. That wasn't going to change, and all the commitments he made to Rick or anyone else would always take second place to the twins and their needs. He just hoped trying to juggle his new client and the twins didn't risk his retaining custody of them. He had to work to feed them, yet his work could make him appear unsuitable. He hoped to God Sarah would be willing to fill in the hours he now needed her.

At the sight of his house, he hit the brakes a little too hard, jolting the sports car to a stop. Bright flowers spilled down either side of his front stoop, one pot turned on its side and its contents trailing down the first step.

"What on earth?" What had Sarah done? His house looked like . . . a home. A cozy cottage filled with a wife and children.

His eyes actually filled with tears. *Tears.* He looked toward the ceiling of his car and blinked to clear his vision. "Don't be a baby, Trent."

He swung out of the car and stopped to look at the crooked flowers. "Just like Mom's," he whispered.

Family was something he'd once had, lost, and lost again and again. He pushed open the front door. As much as he loved Kyle and Caitlin, they'd been thrust upon him. He was terrified of losing them. He couldn't handle any more loss. The more people he allowed himself to love, the more chance of getting hurt again.

"I'm back."

Silence greeted him. His heart skipped a beat with worry.

"Hello?" He threw his keys onto the small table just inside the front door.

He found Caitlin, Kyle, and Sarah curled up on his bed asleep. A singing mermaid played on his TV/VCR combo. Sarah lay with a child on each side, her hair spread out like a halo beneath her.

"Sarah?" he whispered. Part of him hated to wake her, but another part knew that if he didn't get her out of his bed that minute, the careful control he kept on his emotions would erupt.

"Trent?" She opened her eyes, a dreamy smile on her lips. Easing the twins off her arms, she slid down the middle of the bed and off the end.

He tried his best not to notice the way her body rippled with the motion. And he definitely didn't notice the sexy tumble of curls across her shoulders or how moist and kissable her lips looked. Not him. His control was solid. A rock.

She followed him into the living room. "How did the meeting go?"

He shrugged. "Not well."

She laid a hand on his arm. "I'm sorry." She lowered her lashes.

Mercy. Didn't she realize what she was doing to him? He wanted to pull her into his arms and kiss her until she screamed his name.

"Word of my frequent absences from work sites is starting to get around." He scowled, loosened his necktie, and threw it on the bed. "But believe it or not, Matthews offered to give me a chance. I have a feeling

I'd better not be one second late."

"Maybe once you hire that nanny things will settle down."

"Except that I didn't find *one* decent candidate."

"Not even one?" She chewed on her lower lip. He'd like to help her nibble it, but he couldn't and keep his distance.

"We'll manage. Thanks for your help today, Sarah." He had to get her out of his house. What would she think if he swept her up and kissed her senseless?

"About that." She crossed one foot over the other and then back again. "I was thinking maybe I could be their nanny for a while."

"You?"

"I'm not exactly Frankenstein's monster." She crossed her arms.

"I didn't mean that, it's just that—" Just that to have her around every day and not be able to touch her would drive him insane.

"Just that what?" Sarah's blue eyes narrowed dangerously.

Now he'd hurt her feelings. He wasn't one of those smooth-talking types. He always seemed to jam his foot in as far as it would go.

"Well, what about your dog training?"

"What about it? Right now, I only have a few clients. I could train them with the kids right there or when you get home. My business tends to be seasonal, and I'm still in the process of building it up. Summer and Christmas are big times for puppy training. And I can fit in any new clients around your schedule."

"It's too much to ask, Sarah." She would be putting her life on hold for two children who weren't hers. "With this new job I'm going to need someone to watch the kids from seven in the morning until well after dinner. I have to be on the site a lot at the start of a new job and still monitor other jobs my crews are working on."

"Look, Trent. I'm extremely fond of Kyle and Caitlin, and I can't bear the thought of some maniac watching them. Today was—" She spread her hands. "Magical. Give me a chance."

It would be next to impossible to keep his hands off of her on a daily basis.

"I work late hours sometimes," he warned. Maybe he should get a nine-to-five office job and close the construction company. The long hours could very well be the element that would cause him to lose the kids to Nathan Winters. He'd do anything to keep that from happening. But he wasn't sure what else he could do. He'd always been in construction.

"As long as I have a general idea of the schedule, that'll be fine," Sarah said.

"The twins are two handfuls."

"I've seen them in action."

"I'm a handful."

"I've seen you in action, too." She grinned.

His attraction to Sarah would be torture, but he needed a nanny.

"You've got a job, Sarah Goldwyne." She would be good for the twins. Good to the twins.

"I'll see you early Monday morning, Trent Kasey."

Caitlin cried, lunch burned, and Kyle pulled the tape out of a video and draped it all over the living room. Eleven o'clock. Only six or seven more hours until Trent got home.

She sat down in his armchair and rested her head on her hands. Keep up with twins? She'd have to be ten years

38

younger and ten times faster.

" 'Arah." Kyle patted her arm.

She forced a smile and raised her head. A tiny frown puckered his forehead, and his thumb had found its way to his mouth. Caitlin clutched her blankie and stared at Sarah with wide eyes.

"Come here, you rascals." She scooped Kyle onto her lap and Caitlin followed.

" 'ove, 'Arah." Kyle planted a slobbery kiss on her cheek.

"Did you just say you love me?" Sarah's heart lurched with love for the tiny child.

"Me tooooo." Caitlin drawled out the word into an extra syllable.

If it took her the rest of the day to clean up their mess, it was worth it to hear the twins say they loved her. Oh, it would hurt when Trent eventually found someone he wanted to marry and Sarah was no longer a part of their lives. Losing the twins would hurt. Losing Trent might hurt even more.

She pushed that thought away.

"Let's clean up this mess and go over to my house. I have a poodle coming for obedience training. What do you think?"

"Doggie." Caitlin's eyes lit up.

Kyle clapped his hands.

It was going to be tough to keep up with the twins and her dog trainer business at the same time, but even in her off season she couldn't afford to lose regular clients like the Van Horns.

Trent bent over and picked up a crushed bright pink flower from the walkway. What had happened to the flowers? He frowned. Petals lay scattered amid clumps of dirt.

He'd remember to ask Sarah later. Right now he just wanted to see the twins. To hold them. He hadn't seen them for ten hours. This was the first time they'd been apart for more than an hour or two since he'd brought them home after his sister's funeral.

A tornado, nuclear holocaust, and earthquake had hit his living room. One cushion from the couch lay on the floor. Toys trailed across the room and toward the kitchen. Bits of paper covered his tan carpet. Kyle. He hoped Sarah didn't quit on the spot. He winced and followed the paper trail into the kitchen.

"Kyle, you little rascal." She was on her hands and knees on the floor scrubbing bright red goo. "I turn my back for one minute. Not two but one—and you do this?" She laughed softly.

"Looks like you had a busy day."

She jumped. "You're early."

"Is that an accusation?"

Her eyes glittered dangerously. Uh-oh. He couldn't handle tears.

"I was kidding, Sarah. What happened?"

"It was Kyle. I just turned my back for one minute to check on dinner. He's been really good lately, so I didn't think—I mean who would think one child could make such a mess in *one* minute? I'm so sorry. I'll get everything cleaned up. Don't fire me," she finished in a breathless rush.

"Want some help?" Trent took the sponge out of her hand, dipped it into the nearby bucket of soapy water, and knelt to scrub at the goo on the floor.

"Trent Kasey, you are truly the most amazing man I've ever met."

The look in her eyes was definitely fond. Time to put on the brakes. Couldn't allow either of them to care too much. It would only create heartache later. The last thing in the world he wanted was for Sarah to be hurt. The second to last thing he wanted was to be hurt himself.

"What is this anyway?" He pointed to the red goo on the floor.

"My first cherry pie ever. I'm not a great cook, but I thought I'd attempt it."

"I'll bet it was the best pie I've never had."

She leaned over and whispered, "The truth is that Kyle, who will gobble down anything, wouldn't even eat it. He took one bite, spit it out, and left the rest lying there."

He laughed. "At least you tried."

She stared at him for a moment and backed up a few steps. "I'm going to go now. Dinner is on the stove. The twins have had a bath."

"Thanks, Sarah." He'd gotten home fairly early that night. He watched Sarah back out of the kitchen and wondered what it might be like if she headed for his bedroom instead of her own house. He shook his head to chase those thoughts away. He didn't have time for a relationship and the complications involved.

Chapter Five

Each day with the twins filled the empty hole in Sarah's heart a little more, but she knew it would never be totally filled.

"Maybe if they were mine to raise." She sighed. She'd decided after that busy first day to stop second-guessing life. She would enjoy her time with the twins for as long as she was allowed and be thankful for the experience.

"Bedtime, guys." She'd made it through the first week. Tonight was Trent's late night; he wouldn't be home until after nine. She planned to fit in new clients on Saturdays or another day during the week to accommodate his schedule.

She tucked the twins in, read them *Sleeping Beauty*, and kissed the top of each silky, dark head.

Then she did it. She made the mistake of phoning her mother.

"Where have you been? I've been calling and calling. I thought you'd walked right into the ocean and drowned."

"Mom, please. I'm fine."

Silence stretched on the other end. She collapsed onto the repaired sofa cushion and tucked her feet under her.

"There's a man, isn't there, Sarah?"

Her mother's voice sounded so hopeful that Sarah almost wished there were a romance between her and Trent. But what point was there in leading her mother on? Nothing serious could ever come from her attraction to Trent.

"Well?"

"Actually, there is. He's about two feet tall and his name is Kyle."

"What?"

She twirled the cord.

"I'm helping a neighbor. I'm nanny to twins."

"You're kidding, right?" *Tap tap tap.*

What was that noise? She held the phone from her ear.

"No, Mom. I'm really enjoying it."

"Well, if you ask me—"

"Which I didn't," she pointed out.

"—instead of watching some other woman's happy family, you should be out meeting men your age." Her mother continued as though Sarah hadn't even interrupted. *Tap tap tap.*

The scrape of Trent's key in the front door alerted Sarah to his arrival.

"Mom, I have to go—"

"I just want you to be happy, Sarah. Is that too much to ask? I want all my children to be happy."

She rolled her eyes. Her mother could go on for hours once she started the I-want-my-children-to-be-happy speech. It was time to get off the phone so that she didn't have to explain a man's voice to her mother.

"Do you remember Mary Parker? Her son is about your age . . ."

"Don't even think about it, Mom. I still remember the last time you tried to fix Ryan up." The front door swung inward, Trent's broad shoulders outlined in the doorway. "I have to go, Mom."

"Ryan is another lecture. I'm talking about you, Sarah. Dogs are good company, but they can't keep you warm on a lonely night."

"Hello." His husky voice reached across the room and

wrapped around her like a warm blanket. She swallowed and gripped the phone a bit tighter as he shut the front door and crossed the room.

"Who is that?" Her mother had apparently heard Trent's voice.

Tight jeans stretched across his muscular thighs, and his blue shirt was unbuttoned halfway down. She wondered if he knew how sexy he looked. A large mark of grease splattered across one shoulder. It only added to his rugged look, making Sarah want to strip his shirt off and lead him to the shower.

"Sarah Ann Goldwyne!" Her mother's voice screeched across the lines. "Tell me you aren't interested in a married man."

She grinned. Let her mother go insane with worry. Served her right for meddling so much. "I need to go now, Mom. Time for bed. G'night." She laid the phone back in the cradle.

"Sorry I'm so late." Trent sank down onto the sofa next to her.

He laid his head back against the couch, closed his eyes, and stretched his long legs out, his thigh brushing against hers.

She sucked in her breath and held it. Fire licked across her body where his leg touched hers. He opened his brilliant green eyes and slid one hand slowly down her arm. She bit her lip to keep from moaning with pleasure.

"Everything going okay with the twins?"

"The twins are amazing." Her voice wobbled a bit. *Just great, Sarah. Why don't you just tell him you think he's hotter than an active volcano?*

"I have a custody hearing a week from next Friday."

She sat up straight, her body stiffening.

"Didn't I mention that before?"

"No," Sarah shouted.

"The twins' biological father wants custody."

"Why didn't you tell me? I didn't even realize there was a father in the picture."

"There never has been. He only crawled out of the woodwork when he realized he might be able to blackmail me for some money. I know I was a royal jerk not to tell you, but I tried to put it out of my mind."

"He never married your sister?" Sarah wondered what Trent would say if she told him she knew *exactly* how Melissa must have felt.

"No. He seduced her and when she told him she was pregnant, he disappeared."

"That's terrible." At least Paul hadn't disappeared, although sometimes she thought it might have been better if he had.

"She was too trusting, even at twenty-five. He fooled her. Lied to her. Told her he loved her." Trent rubbed his hand over his eyes. "With our parents dead, she only had me to turn to. I helped her the best I could, but I may have sheltered her too much. Melissa was forced to grow up after Nathan left her, and look at the world and those around with less trust."

"If he's never been in their lives, why does there even have to be a court hearing?" Sarah asked.

"It's no big deal." Trent didn't meet her gaze, and Sarah wondered just how big a deal the upcoming hearing was. "Just a formality."

"You're sure?" Sarah asked

"It's going to be fine," he said. It was what Sarah wanted to hear, so she didn't press the issue further.

"Have I told you lately what a great job you're doing?" he asked.

"Not lately." Warmth spread through her. If she closed her eyes tight, she could imagine that they were husband and wife having a typical end-of-evening conversation, and Kyle and Caitlin were her children sleeping peacefully in the next room.

He waved something in front of her face, bringing her out of her trance. "Your salary."

She swallowed. Nothing like reality slapping you out of your dream. She took the money, but her hand felt grungy and dirty where she touched the bills.

"I feel guilty taking this, I have so much fun with the kids."

"You earned it." His arm rested across the back of the couch, one hand curling around her shoulder. He leaned toward her a bit as though he might kiss her or was at least thinking about it.

She jumped from the couch. "I need to go."

"Why so skittish, Sarah?"

"This isn't happening, Trent. You're lonely. I'm lonely. We both love the twins. That doesn't mean we're going to fall into bed together. I already told you that I can't handle another broken heart. I'm still not healed from the last time."

"Who said anything about bed?" He glanced down at the couch. The smoldering look in his eyes spoke loudly that he would have her right there in the living room given the chance.

"No way, Trent. Not in this lifetime." She slammed the front door behind her. Trent Kasey was determined to break her heart.

Not in this lifetime. Sarah's words echoed through his head long after she'd left.

"We'll see about that, Sarah Goldwyne."

Chapter Six

"You're going to lose." Nathan Winters's stale breath filled the air as he hissed his hateful words on his way out of the courtroom.

"This is never going to be over." Trent slumped into the heavy, slat-backed chair and steepled his fingers against his forehead.

Gregg Roberts tapped his papers into place, snapped the locks on his briefcase, clicked his tongue twice, and then said, "Be thankful they didn't make a decision today."

His head shot up, and he glared at his lawyer. He was a good parent to the twins. He planned to raise them the way his sister would have wanted, and he loved them with every fiber of his being. Had loved them from the moment they'd been born and each tiny fist had clasped one of his little fingers on either hand. His love had blossomed on that day and continued to grow with each breath Caitlin and Kyle had taken.

"Can't the judge see that Winters doesn't love them?" He couldn't believe a judge, a learned man with years of experience, would fall for Nathan Winters's syrupy sweet doting father act. The man had never even seen the twins.

"You know that and I know that, buddy. The judge just sees a father."

He sighed. "What can I do to get a good recommendation from the investigator?"

"Make sure the kids are clean, house is clean . . ." Gregg paused.

"Anything, Gregg. I'll do whatever it takes."

"Traditionally, parents are given more weight. You have an advantage because you've had the children for three months and Winters hasn't been in their lives and your sister named you in her will. You have two major disadvantages. Your sister failed to terminate the father's rights, and the twins are too young to tell the judge they want to stay with you."

"Odds. I need odds." He'd leave the country. Pack up and go to Austria or somewhere. Nathan Winters, the abusive bastard who'd thrown money at his sister and told her to get an abortion, would not raise Caitlin and Kyle.

"Odds are eighty-twenty."

"That's not bad." He relaxed.

"Against you, buddy."

His heart thumped hard enough to break a rib.

"Fifty-fifty if you get married."

"I told you—"

"And I'm telling you. You want to keep those kids, elope to Vegas."

Gregg Roberts snatched his briefcase off the table and left the courtroom with the muted thump of designer dress shoes.

Who could he marry in the three weeks until the court-appointed investigator's visit? The name that popped into his head didn't surprise him. Sarah. Yeah right. She wanted kids about as much as he wanted a wife right now. Sure she enjoyed having them a few hours each day, but she'd never given any indication that she wanted to be a full-time nanny and wife. Actually, she'd mentioned more than once that she didn't want to get involved with him. He'd love to punch the man who'd hurt her, but instead he'd have to focus on convincing her to change her mind.

★ ★ ★ ★ ★

One tiny set of bright blue eyes stared at Sarah over the hedge she trimmed.

"Hello." She ruffled Kyle's dark curls. It wasn't fair that a boy had such gorgeous hair and eyelashes.

" 'Ewwo."

"Hey, I understood that." She smiled at the boy. "Where is your sister?"

Kyle stared at her.

"Hmmm . . . you haven't run off again, have you?" She glanced around, but there was no sign of Trent Kasey. It was Saturday, and she was on her own. She'd just been thinking how lonely she was without the twins or their sexy uncle for company. "I'll just bet you have, you little raga-muffin."

Walking around to the other side of the hedge, Sarah scooped the boy into her arms and allowed herself to hold his warm body close for just a moment. He wrapped his arms around her neck and gave her a noisy kiss on the cheek. Sarah's heart thudded with longing. If only he were hers to keep. To tuck in every night. No sense thinking like that. It wasn't going to happen.

She settled Kyle firmly on her hip and set off with a determined stride toward the house next door. While she loved Kyle's company, it was important for the children to understand that she might not be a permanent fixture in their lives no matter how much she might want to be. It would save them heartache later. She knocked firmly on the door.

After a few minutes, Trent cracked the door open. His eyes were bloodshot, and his hair stood up in tufts.

"You look awful," she blurted.

"Thanks. Glad I made an impression."

Sarah felt warmth flood her cheeks. "Are you sick?"

"I never get sick."

She eyed his flushed cheeks suspiciously. "Did you know Kyle was in the yard by himself?"

"Oh, God." He slung the door open and snatched the boy out of her arms. "Kyle. You can't do this to Uncle Trent right now. What if the social worker came and you were outside by yourself?"

"What social worker? Does this have something to do with that custody hearing?"

He stared at her for a moment before turning and walking back into the house. "If you want to hear this story, you'd better come in. It's a long one."

She followed him inside. She shrugged. She'd always been too curious for her own good. Maybe she could watch the twins just for a short while so he could get some rest. It had to be hard adjusting to the weekends and not having her help. Oh, who was she trying to fool? She wanted an excuse to be around Trent on the weekends, too, even if it only lasted a few hours.

"Have you eaten today?"

"No. I managed to fix the twins cereal for lunch."

"I'm cooking you soup." She headed for the kitchen.

Trent and the twins followed her. She searched through cabinets until she found a family-size can of chicken noodle soup and a large pot. She opened the can, poured the soup into the pot, and placed each twin in a high chair.

"I can tell you've been practicing on the twins. You're efficient."

"You have to be with two."

"Why aren't you married, Sarah?"

She sucked in her breath. That was one place she most definitely didn't want to go. She could barely stand the thought of not being able to have children herself. She certainly didn't want to share that thought with Trent. Besides, she wasn't ready for him to get that cold, withdrawn look in his eyes yet. She knew it wasn't totally fair, but she enjoyed that faint gleam of male appreciation as he took in her short gardening cutoffs or the way his thigh brushed against hers when he sat next to her on the couch.

"You were going to tell me about the social worker."

He sighed. "Nice change of subject."

"I don't want to talk about it yet."

"Fair enough. As I mentioned before, Kyle and Caitlin's biological father wants custody."

She frowned. She didn't see what was so wrong with the man wanting to see his children, although she felt they belonged with Trent. Even a selfish man like Nathan Winters could love a child.

"Surely you can work something out on visitation?"

"Never." His jaw clenched, and his voice was clipped.

"Maybe he's changed, Trent. Why wouldn't he love those two? They are wonderful."

"If Nathan Winters loved them, why has he been absent from their lives from the first moment my sister announced she was pregnant? He doesn't even know them."

"That's sad."

"He told me two months ago when I contacted him to let him know Melissa had died that he would sign a document giving up any rights to the children if I would give him ten thousand dollars. He would give up those kids for so little. When I refused, he decided he wanted to contest Melissa's wishes that I raise the children."

"That's horrible." She grabbed a soup ladle and stirred the soup rapidly.

"I told you there was a hearing on Friday . . ."

"Then you won." Sarah felt like cheering. The twins were so sweet, if mischievous. They deserved someone who loved them the way Trent obviously did.

"No. There was a continuance so that the judge could order home study. I could still lose them."

She wondered for a moment if he looked so dejected because he was sick or because the twins might go live with their father. The glance he sent their way answered that question. He wouldn't be able to bear losing the children. They seemed to mean everything to him. She wondered how *she*'d be able to face the day if the twins went to live with their father. Goose bumps erupted on her arms. She didn't even want to think about it.

"Just get a good report on the home study." She shrugged. Should be simple. The twins were happy.

"I plan to. There's one major problem."

"You're a good father to them, Trent. I'll be glad to testify to that." She stirred the soup again.

"I have a major drawback. My odds aren't good."

"Your job?"

"That's partly it. The construction company is growing by leaps and bounds. I can barely keep up. But that isn't the only reason."

"Well, what else could it be? Do you have a disease or something?" Really. Did the man have to be so mysterious?

She leaned over the table to set the soup in front of him. As she pulled back her arm brushed against his. Heat flooded through her body. Need and want all rolled into one sensation. She pulled away as quickly as she could and sat down in the chair across from Trent.

"Yeah. It's called being single."

She winced. It couldn't be helped. She now had to ask the question, and once she asked it he'd have a right to demand her answer in return.

"Why aren't you married, Trent?"

"There was never a reason to be until now."

Trent waited for Sarah's reaction. She chewed her lower lip and twisted a strand of tawny hair. He left out the fact that he'd been engaged once to his high school sweetheart. Those were memories he'd just as soon forget. It seemed nearly everyone he'd ever loved had died.

"You have someone in mind?"

Did she suspect that it was her? He took a breath to steady his nerves. She had already given up so much of her life just to care for the twins, and she was still a stranger in many ways. He had no right to ask her to put her life on hold and help him out. No right at all. But he was going to do it anyway. There really wasn't a choice. He couldn't risk losing the twins.

"Someone, yes."

Sarah's smile looked a little strained. Her chin trembled almost imperceptibly.

"I hope it works out for you, Trent. Let me know if there's anything I can do." A jack-in-the-box couldn't have stood up faster. She edged toward the door. "I really need to get going—"

"Wait!" Was that his voice that sounded so desperate?

" 'Arah!" Kyle tugged at the hem of her shorts to get her attention.

His eyes fell to that supershort hem and traveled down the length of those sinfully long legs. Have mercy. He needed her help and all he could think of was her legs.

"I need to go, munchkin. I'll see you Monday." She stroked Kyle's dark hair.

As she turned, he thought he saw a glint of moisture on

the tips of her eyelashes. The door closed softly behind her. What was wrong with him? His plea for her to marry him had been the next step.

He'd wimped out. Something he couldn't afford to do if he wanted to keep the twins out of Nathan Winters's greedy grasp. Perhaps he should just sign some money over. He wasn't rich, but he could afford to send the twins to college and ensure their futures were bright, unless he was forced to pay off Nathan Winters. It would get Nathan Winters out of their lives, so it might be worth it to pay the man off and worry about money for college later.

Everything within him screamed against the idea. It was the one thing his sister had been adamant about. She hadn't wanted Winters to get his hands on that life insurance money. He sighed. But Melissa wasn't there to deal with the heartache. How would he survive if the court took the twins away?

"Stupid, Sarah. Really, really stupid." She let Nightfire tug her along with the leash. The jog to keep up with the frolicky puppy was meant to clear her head. Instead, she felt more confused than before.

Had she actually believed he might ask her to marry him? She laughed, the sound catching in her throat. Of course he would have someone in mind. And that someone wasn't her. What if his new wife didn't want her to care for the kids anymore? Could she bear it?

A sob tore through her throat, and she shouted a halt to Night's run. The dog turned back and looked at her with a puzzled frown on his face. Okay, maybe dogs didn't feel puzzlement, but Sarah didn't know how else to explain the look.

Sinking into the soft, warm sand, Sarah drew her knees

up and wrapped her arms around them. Crazy to get so emotional over a man she'd known for such a short period of time.

Maybe she should marry an older man. Someone more established. Someone who didn't want children at such a late stage of life. But even as the thought presented itself, she knew it wasn't likely. To her, marriage meant a family. Perhaps it was that she had three brothers. Perhaps it was that she so desperately wanted a child of her own. Perhaps it was part of her inherent nature. Whatever the cause, her heart told her that children were an integral part of marriage.

Trent already had two children to raise. Maybe—

She jumped to her feet, startling Nightfire, who scrambled away from her. "Maybe nothing. Maybe my fairy godmother will float down from the sky and rescue me from the wicked infertility stepmother."

Tiny bursts of sand wriggled into her shoes as she stomped down the beach. She welcomed the discomfort. It was proof that she was alive and real. She really had to get over this obsession with the children. Needed to learn to be thankful for the time she did have with Caitlin and Kyle. Life could be worse. She could never know the laughter of a child at all. Without the twins, her world would be barren of that tinkly laughter.

She returned from her walk to madness and mayhem. News vans and camera crews filled Trent's lawn and had tumbled over onto hers.

"Jenna Cox with Channel Fourteen News. A heartbroken father fights for custody of the children he loves."

She tried to slip up the path to her house, but one of the reporters spotted her.

"Miss! Miss! A quote please."

"I really don't think—"

"Just a short one?" The woman's toothy smile was the white of professionally bleached teeth.

"What's going on here?" Trent stepped out onto his porch and into the bright glare of the lights.

She barely held back a groan. It was obvious that he needed help with this situation. It wasn't her place to get involved. She was just the nanny. She shouldn't allow herself to care. She was going to step into the ring anyway.

"Trent!" She waved.

He frowned. She made her way quickly to his side.

"Watch every word," she muttered from the side of her mouth.

"I demand to see my children," Nathan Winters bellowed.

She wondered if Trent had judged the man incorrectly. Perhaps he truly did love Caitlin and Kyle.

"Tell them what you really want, Winters," Trent growled.

"Easy," Sarah whispered.

"Uncle Trent?" Caitlin and Kyle opened the door behind him.

Trent groaned.

"My babies." Nathan Winters turned to the cameras, tears coursing freely down his face.

She frowned. If he loved them so much, why was he rushing toward the cameras rather than the children? Why hadn't he called even once to check on the children?

"Miss, who are you?" A young male reporter shoved his microphone under her nose.

"The nanny."

"A live-in nanny?" the reporter asked with a suggestive wink.

"No. I rent the house next door."

"Do you think the twins should be allowed to see their father?" another reporter yelled.

"Sarah doesn't know Nathan Winters or his greed." Trent crossed his arms defensively.

"Sarah? Do you believe the children are getting what they need from Mr. Kasey?"

"He loves them very much. It's obvious."

"Is that why he leaves them with a nanny?" the snide reporter asked.

"Mr. Kasey has to work." She glared at the reporter.

"I just want a few photographs with the children, Trent. Can't you grant a man that?" Nathan again spoke to the cameras.

Trent was gritting his teeth so hard that Sarah could hear a dull grinding sound. "Ten minutes."

The news crews seemed to pack up and disappear. Nathan Winters and a lone photographer stayed behind.

It all seemed so orchestrated. How had the man gotten the news crews to come out here in the first place?

"Why did the reporters come out here, Mr. Winters?" She met his glare without flinching. She'd dealt with bullies before.

"My lawyer sent them a press release. We let them know these children are being kept from their only living parent."

"Some parent," Trent muttered.

"Come give your daddy a kiss, kids." Nathan knelt and motioned the photographer to capture the moment.

"No." Kyle hid behind Trent's legs.

"You've turned them against me."

"They don't know you, Winters. You've never seen them

once in their lives until you thought you might be able to get some money out of me." Trent bent down and soothed a now crying Kyle.

"How about a nice picture with your real father? I'll give you a dollar." Nathan Winters waved the money at them.

The twins, having no concept of money or its purpose, stared at him suspiciously.

"Get over here, you brats. I want some pictures to take back with me."

She gasped. The transformation from potential doting father to thwarted controller was as instantaneous as ice melting under hot water.

Nathan moved toward the children in a threatening manner. Trent stepped forward.

"Lay a hand on them, and you won't make it to the next court hearing."

"Are you threatening me, Kasey?"

"That's right, and I won't color it over for any reporters. Now get off my property."

Winters's mouth stretched into a semblance of a smile, as though his mouth had forgotten the exact muscles needed to complete the movement. "I'll see you in court, Kasey. Good luck. You'll need it."

Chapter Seven

"Stay, Nightfire." She held her hand up and backed away slowly.

Night crawled forward on his belly, following her.

"No. Stay." She backed away two more steps.

Night followed on his belly. She stopped. Night wagged his tail, panted twice, and bounded to his feet, running to her side.

She laughed. "What am I going to do with you?"

She didn't believe in using choker chains or raising her voice to the animals. Although some trainers used those methods, Sarah had found that with extra patience most animals would respond to a gentler training.

"Heel." She walked back to the spot where Night had started.

"Wab Wa." Kyle's tiny face peeked through a gap in the hedge.

She had no clue what Kyle had just said, but he was looking at the dog. "Hi, Kyle. I'm training Nightfire. Want to watch?"

Kyle nodded and slipped through the hedge. He stood beside her, mocking her movements.

"Night, stay." She backed up a step. Kyle backed up a step. Night followed.

"No. Stay." Another step away from the friendly dog.

" 'tay!" Kyle told the dog.

Night bounded to the boy and licked his face. Kyle fell to the ground, giggling.

"Heel, Night." She walked the dog back to the starting point.

" 'tay?" Kyle asked.

She laughed. "Exactly. Look, Kyle. It worked this time. Nightfire is staying put."

"Hey, champ. Today is Sarah's day off." Trent stood on the other side of the hedge. "I was looking for you."

"You seem to spend a lot of time doing that."

He smiled, a slow sexy smile that made Sarah's heart miss a beat. "Think you could train Kyle to stay?"

"Are you kidding? I can't even train my dog."

Sarah's gaze flew to his left hand. Ring finger still bare. Relief rushed through her, making her dizzy. Still single. Not that it made any difference as far as she was concerned. She was just the nanny. No sense in daydreaming about anything else.

"Listen, Sarah, I wanted to talk to you about—"

"Twent!" Caitlin tackled Trent from behind, pushing him into the hedge.

"Looks like you have your hands full, and I need to get back to work with Nightfire. It's not good business when your own dog doesn't know how to behave. I haven't spent enough time training him lately. It takes a lot of practice and patience." She turned her attention back to Night.

He stared at her for a moment before taking a child's hand in each of his and walking slowly toward his house. He turned back to look at her once, as though there was something more he wanted to say.

He would fire her. She scrubbed at the gooey eggs with bits of shell stuck in the middle.

"Kyle, buddy. Next time you want eggs, just ask, okay?"

"Okay." Kyle blew her a kiss.

She laughed. "Okay, charmer. You're forgiven."

"Sarah!" The front door slammed behind Trent's shout.

"In the kitchen."

"Come here."

She frowned. "There's no need to shout—" she broke off as she walked into the living room and saw Princess, a chow mix she was training, chewing on Trent's sofa cushion.

"Princess, how did you get in here?" She dropped to her knees and pulled the fabric from the dog's mouth. Princess didn't let go, and the sound of ripping fabric filled the room.

She looked up at him. His face was red, and a vein throbbed rapidly in his left temple. She watched in fascination. The only other time she'd ever seen Trent get angry was with Nathan Winters, and that had been an icy fury. This was a blazing fury, full of passion. Call her insane but any show of passion from him would be welcome as far as she was concerned.

"I'll have the couch reupholstered." She rose to her feet and stepped closer. "I've never seen you this angry."

"Sarah, get that dog out of my house, or I won't be responsible for what happens to her."

She clicked her tongue. "Violence? Toward an innocent animal?"

"Why is the dog in my house? And whose dog is it?"

"This is Princess. She's a client of mine. As to how she got in the house . . ." Sarah saw Kyle dart behind the recliner. "I have my theories."

He raised his arm and pointed to the door. "Out."

Sarah's heart thudded in her chest. Did he mean her or the dog? He was furious. She knew what trouble Kyle could get into. While she'd been cleaning up one mess, he'd been getting into something else. Why hadn't she made him stay

61

in the kitchen with her? The thought of spending her days without the twins, or the sound of his key in the front door, brought tears to her eyes.

"Are you firing me?"

"What?" He frowned. "No. I just want the dog out."

"Okay." She grabbed Princess's collar and led her out the door.

He shouldn't have been so harsh with her. Yes, the dog was a beast. But Sarah had a soft spot for animals, and he knew that. The couch could be replaced. She couldn't. He allowed that thought to sink in for a moment. Then he lied to himself, knowing it was a lie, but not caring.

"Because she's a good nanny. That's the only reason."

Tears had glistened on her lashes before she'd bent down to grab the dog's collar. The last thing he wanted was to hurt Sarah. He knew how it felt to get burned with the brunt of someone's anger, knowing you weren't really at fault. Okay, maybe Sarah was at fault, but it was just a couch.

"Just a lousy couch, and I made her cry." He grabbed his car keys. "Caitlin, Kyle. Let's go bye-bye."

Two dark heads peeked around the kitchen doorway. "Bye-bye?"

She drove the spade into the weed with enough force to take out the flowers on either side of it. She pushed the flowers back into place, knowing she'd killed them. She brushed tears from her cheeks.

"He's not going to make me cry." She sniffed.

Princess licked her arm.

"I'm mad at you too."

Princess whined.

"Don't give me that. You destroyed the man's couch. I'll be lucky if he doesn't fire me. And if he does, you just watch out because I'll be horrible to be around. Miserable."

She'd been chastising Princess when Trent and the twins rushed from the house and left in his Camaro. Maybe he was going to look for a new nanny. Or maybe he was going to see the woman he planned to marry? Night lay on her porch, behaving himself for once.

"What if she wants the kids to herself? He may not need a nanny any longer."

An hour later, the sound of Trent's car pulling back into the gravel drive caught Sarah's attention. Sarah continued to tear stubborn weeds from the earth, feeling sorry for herself.

Don't look up. What if she is with him?

Two brown shoes came into her line of vision. "Sarah?"

Please don't let him introduce me to her. I don't want to meet his future wife.

She looked up. He was alone except for the twins. No woman in sight. She smiled, knowing it was too wide a smile for the circumstances and not caring. He was alone.

"I'm not good with words." He held out a handful of mixed flowers. "I'm sorry I yelled."

She took the flowers and buried her face in them to hide the tears that coursed freely down her cheeks now. Flowers? A man had never brought her flowers. Her mother had chosen even the corsage for her prom.

"Sarah? Are you crying?"

"Only a little." She lifted her face and smiled at him. "You're forgiven."

He laughed. "That was easy."

"I'm an easy girl." She shrugged.

"Is that so?" His lips crooked up into a suggestive smile.

She felt her cheeks flush with fire. "I didn't mean. That is—" Oh boy.

"You should probably put those in water, and then I hope you'll have dinner with us. I'm cooking."

"Spaghetti?"

"You got it."

She laughed. "I can't remember when I've received a better offer. I'll be right over."

Did Sarah have any idea what she was doing to him?

She had changed into buttercream, formfitting khakis and a soft, wispy-looking sweater.

"Amber Jenkins is the local seamstress. She'll be over tomorrow to give me an estimate on your couch."

"Fine. No big deal."

"I'm really sorry."

He motioned for her to sit down and sat next to her. "No. I'm sorry for being such a jerk."

"It was understandable."

"There's never an excuse for being abusive."

She laid a hand on his arm. "You were hardly abusive. Surely you don't think that?"

"Sometimes I wonder. I had a rough childhood."

"I thought your parents—"

"They died when I was twelve."

"I knew they were gone, but I didn't know you were orphaned so young. I'm so sorry." She lifted her hand hesitantly, then brushed her fingers through the hair at his temples. He sucked in his breath and grabbed her hand with his own to prevent her from touching him any further. He was going to throw her down on the floor and—

"Twent!" Caitlin tugged at his sleeve. "Drink."

"I'll get it." She jumped to her feet. "You talk."

"Melissa was only eleven. No one wanted to take us in. We bounced from relative to relative. Then Cousin Steve came along."

He followed Sarah to the kitchen. She poured apple juice into a sipper cup and handed it to Caitlin.

"Cousin Steve took you in?"

"He took us all right. Took us for every penny in our trust funds. Took us for the fools we were. Took our childhood."

She sank into a chair at the kitchen table. He wasn't sure why he was telling her about his childhood. It was something he had tried to erase from his memory. Perhaps he felt he owed her an explanation after blowing up earlier.

"Steve went to court to get custody and be appointed the legal representative of our trusts. Only there was no one willing to fight for us."

"Trent, I'm sorry. Did he hit you?"

"No. Even at twelve I wouldn't have stood for that. Especially where Melissa was concerned. She was all I had." His voice broke, and he cleared his throat.

"Verbal abuse. Calling us good-for-nothing. The trust money was supposed to pay for our college. When it came time for me to go, I discovered Steve had spent every last cent."

He paced to the other end of the kitchen.

"What did you do, Trent?"

"I found a job in construction and put Melissa through school." He left out the part where he'd waited for the day he could open his own business and make a decent profit so he could ask his high school sweetheart to marry him and three days later she'd taken enough pills to kill an elephant, never mind a wisp of a girl.

"You were a wonderful brother."

He turned back to where she sat, leaned over, and placed his hands on the kitchen table. "I won't let Nathan Winters have the kids or their money. He isn't going to do to them what Steve did to Melissa and me. Melissa wouldn't allow it, and neither will I."

She placed her hands over his and gazed up at him. "We won't let him."

We. For so long he had been singular. Him against the world. Him against Nathan Winters. Him against the encroaching loneliness. *We* sounded like a nice change.

"Did you ask her yet?" she asked.

"Ask who what?" He stared at her mouth.

She wet her lips nervously, but when he swallowed she immediately stopped.

"Ask the woman of your dreams to marry you?" Were they on a different wavelength?

"Not yet." He leaned closer.

His lips were close enough that if she leaned forward a little, or even rose from her chair, they'd be kissing. She looked down. It wouldn't be very smart to kiss an almost married man.

"When is your appointment with the social worker?" She cleared her throat, then chanced looking up at him.

He'd straightened, his mouth no longer mere inches from hers.

"Two weeks."

"Don't you think you'd better let your lady in on your idea?" She tapped the face of the watch on her wrist. "The clock is ticking."

"Actually, I wanted to talk to you about that."

"You did?" She felt her heart flutter for a moment. What if he'd changed his mind about asking the woman to marry him?

"You're doing a great job as nanny, Sarah."

"Oh." She felt hope deflate like a balloon with a leak. "Thank you."

"I don't want to risk losing you."

She narrowed her eyes. In other words, he wanted to have his cake—the new wife—and eat it too—keep Sarah as the kids' nanny. She would say no, except she was already crazy about Caitlin and Kyle.

"Why don't we just see how things work out? Your wife may not want another woman around."

He frowned and looked utterly bewildered. Well, it had been his suggestion in the first place. What did he expect? Probably that she would fall all over herself to accommodate him. Something she seemed prone to. Well, she'd made the mistake of living to please Paul when she was younger. It wasn't a mistake she was likely to repeat.

"I have to go, Trent." She rose from the table, knocked her chair over backwards, righted it, and edged for the front door.

"Sarah, wait, I wanted to talk to you about—"

She cut him off. "Can we chat later? I'm really worried about Princess."

Skillfully avoiding making a commitment to stay on after the new wife came to live with Trent, Sarah rushed out the door and ducked into her house. Thank God it was Friday, and she wouldn't have to see him until Monday. Hopefully by then he'd have forgotten all about adding her to his mishmash family.

Chapter Eight

Time was running out, not with the gentle tick tock of a grandfather clock but with the blare of a five-dollar alarm. The court investigator would arrive a week from tomorrow. Less than eight full days. Trent paced the hardwood floor of the living room, picking up scattered toys along the way.

It had taken him a full week of pep talks and desperation to work up the nerve to discuss marriage with Sarah. Would she be willing to put her life on hold for a few months while he fought Nathan Winters for custody? Would she give more than just the days she'd given them for the last three weeks, but weekends and nights as well?

Last weekend, he'd have thought the answer would be yes. She didn't seem to go out much. He hadn't seen a man around her place, which meant she didn't have a regular boyfriend. If he were a betting man, he would have said the odds of her accepting his crazy proposal were seventy-thirty.

Two days ago, everything changed. The rumble of a heavy diesel engine had drawn him to the front window just as a Ford F250 pickup growled to a stop. She had flown out of the house and thrown herself into the arms of the man stepping down from the running boards. The man had spun her around, and they'd gone into her house arm in arm.

His heart thudded painfully just recalling the look of ecstasy on her face. The man met him in height and was muscled enough to be a body builder. Trent had never been that in shape in his life, and he knew it. Now what was he supposed to do?

He walked to the front window again. Pulling down the slats of the blinds, he stared out at the empty, moonlit driveway next door. It hadn't escaped his notice that the truck had been parked in her driveway for two days. Two days and a night.

Then they'd left, the thunder of the engine drowning out the quiet afternoon nap time. Now, at ten-thirty at night, her driveway was still empty. A weekend away?

"Not your business, Kasey. She isn't on the clock. It's her life."

His foot slammed into the end table. He cursed, then remembered the sleeping twins and bit off what he really wanted to say. Apparently he'd waited too long to ask. Who was this guy anyway? What kind of boyfriend stayed away for weeks, then suddenly appeared?

A strange sensation made his chest tight. *Panic,* he told himself. She had been his one chance of marrying before the hearing. That's all this strange, angry emotion was. Panic. *Where has she gone?*

"Weekend getaway?" His words whispered into the room like foggy tendrils of breath on a cold morning.

Maybe Sarah had just met the guy. She hadn't seemed like the type of woman who would just fall into bed that quickly. He'd seen her as . . . well to be honest . . . more settled. Motherly. Or maybe he'd imputed those attributes to her because that was how he'd wanted her to be.

Vroooooom. The heavy sound of the truck's engine startled him. They were back. He refused to look out the window. None of his business. He had better things to do with his time than spy on his nanny and try to figure out her love life. For one thing, he had to find a wife. In less than eight days.

Maybe he could order one through one of those home

shopping networks. Rush order. He'd pay extra for tawny hair and legs that went on forever. Okay, maybe he'd just take one peek out the window. The red truck sat boldly in her driveway. She and the man had gone inside.

His teeth slammed together with brutal force. He didn't have time for this schoolboy nonsense of wondering what they were doing. He didn't care. It wasn't possible to care in the short period of time he'd known her, so there was no reason to feel a sense of loss. There were other things to worry about. He had to find a wife. Apparently it wasn't going to be Sarah.

"You sure are in a foul mood. Is it because we missed dinner?" Ryan opened her refrigerator, his upper body disappearing inside as he rooted for leftovers.

Sarah opened the freezer above his head, grabbed her emergency stash of Häagen-Dazs double chocolate, and jammed a spoon into it hard enough to bend the flimsy metal handle.

"I'm not in a bad mood."

Ryan polished an apple on his sleeve and straddled one of her oak, barstool chairs. "You can't fool me, Sis. You only eat double chocolate for one of two reasons."

She swallowed the sweet, icy concoction and licked her lips. "You don't know me as well as you think you do. What about you? Care to share the reason for your visit?"

It was Ryan's turn to look uncomfortable. He bit into the apple, spraying a bit of juice across her arm. She wiped it off and glared at him. Ryan just shrugged.

"You don't usually take so long to get to the point, but I'll play. Let's see, you come to see me for one of two reasons. Either you need to borrow money, or your heart's been broken. Since you're no longer in veterinary school but have a successful practice . . . did I mention you still owe me money? . . . I'm assuming it's the heart."

"We know each other too well."

She dug around a crater-size chunk of chocolate and scooped another spoonful of ice cream into her mouth. They said chocolate was a substitute for the emotion of love. She half agreed. In her estimation, love was a substitute for chocolate. Chocolate was easier to get along with, and it didn't bite back like love did.

"So, you gonna tell me who he is first or do I tell you about her first?"

"You first," Sarah said.

Ryan took another bite of apple and chewed. Swallowing, he adopted a casual tone. "Her name is Melody."

"Sounds like a sad song."

"Very funny. I guess I came down here to have you tell me what to do, but on the way I came to my own decision."

"Glad I could be of help."

"Seriously, Sis. I'm going to ask her to marry me."

"Whoa. You? Mr. Confirmed-Bachelor-I-Like-My-Freedom?"

"Melody is special." Ryan abandoned the apple and ran his fingers through his hair.

"She must be spectacular to rate a proposal from you. You're the brother who told me marriage was an institution created to torture unsuspecting souls."

"She's pregnant, Sarah Belle."

Sarah's breath hissed to a stop, and the world turned a fuzzy gray. She forced a smile. This was her brother. The child would be her niece or nephew. She should be thrilled. She *was* thrilled.

"That's wonderful. When's the baby due?" Her smile felt pasty even to her. Envy spiraled through her in ever

71

widening waves. The ripples threatened to drown her in their aftermath. She fought the emotion with an even wider smile.

"You don't have to put a brave face on for me, Sis. I know you, remember?"

"Don't be ridiculous. I'm happy for you. A baby. I'm going to spoil her rotten."

"Sarah, have you ever wondered? What I mean is . . ." Ryan trailed off.

"I wonder all the time, Ryan. It just wasn't meant to be." She shrugged. "It hurts, but I'm starting to come to terms with it. I can't let it define who I am forever."

"Sarah, that was three years ago. Have you gone back to the doctor? Had a second opinion? If I remember correctly, they only said you might not be able to get pregnant again, not that it was a definite."

"Please, Ryan, don't." She set the ice cream aside and swallowed back the salty tears threatening to rise. "There is no point in getting my hopes up. I will never have a child."

Ryan stood and crossed around the breakfast bar to hug her to his chest. "Let it out, baby. Tears heal."

She laid her head on his familiar shoulder, but she didn't want to weep. Instead, she let loose with a string of curses that had her brother blushing. Pent-up anger at the unfairness of a world that granted babies to those who didn't want them and kept them from those who yearned for them came pouring out.

"Feel better?" Ryan asked when the anger was finally spent, and Sarah leaned against him in exhaustion.

"Yes." She grinned. "I hope I didn't scorch your delicate ears."

"Take that anger and turn it into something constructive. Didn't you say your neighbor needed a wife?"

"Don't be ridiculous, Ryan."

"Ridiculous? I'm being practical. He needs a wife. He has two children. You need children to care for like you need air to breathe. You're already crazy about those two. They're all you talk about. The way I see it, you either nanny the rest of your life and have children eight or so hours a day, or you get married and have them twenty-four/seven."

"There's just one little problem. He plans to marry someone else."

"So propose to him. Snatch him out from under her nose. If he's so desperate to keep those kids, he'll marry anyone."

"Thanks a lot." She glared.

"You know what I mean."

Ryan was being ridiculous of course. She could no more propose to Ryan than she could . . . than she could . . . than she could spend the rest of her life alone.

"Do you still need a wife?"

The minute Trent opened the door, Sarah rushed into her breathless question. Her hair waved wildly across the shoulders of a flirty green sundress.

"A wife?"

"To improve your chances of keeping Caitlin and Kyle. Or did you already propose to the lady you had in mind?" Sarah's cheeks flushed a dull rose.

He leaned against the doorframe. "No. The lady had other plans." He pictured the red truck that had been in Sarah's driveway for the last two days. It had rumbled out of sight just a short time ago.

"I have a proposition for you."

He felt his senses slowly crawl to a warm alertness. "Marry me."

The lady had guts. He couldn't imagine what had inspired her to propose, but it couldn't have come at a better time. The social worker's visit was scheduled for Friday.

"Call me traditional, but I always imagined I'd be the one to propose."

She raised her fine, tawny eyebrows, placed one hand on her hip, and looked around the front yard. "I don't see any women crawling through the bushes to accept your proposals."

He hid a smile. He hadn't proposed to anyone yet. He'd still been working up his nerve to propose to her.

"Point taken. In that case, I accept."

She held up her hand. "Two conditions."

Trent couldn't believe they were discussing marriage casually on the doorstep as if she'd just suggested they share cups of sugar if one of them ran out.

"First, when we separate, I still get to see the twins. We work out something on visitations. Perhaps one day a month."

He nodded reluctantly. He didn't want to share the kids with anyone, but he could see the wisdom of her words. They already depended on her. If she came into Kyle and Caitlin's life, then suddenly disappeared, it would be as if they'd lost another mother.

"What's the second condition?"

Sarah's gaze ran leisurely from the tips of his bare toes until her gaze collided with his. He felt warmth crawl up the same path her gaze had.

"Never mind about the second condition. I just changed my mind. We have a flight booked to Las Vegas Monday, and my brother is coming back to watch the kids."

As he watched Sarah's cute little rear end sway back to her own house, he wondered if he'd just imagined their conversation. He whistled as he realized the red pickup must have belonged to her brother. Life was definitely looking up.

"Yoo-hoo."

She cringed. No. It couldn't be. It wasn't her—mother.

"Mom? What are you doing here?"

Catherine threw her arms around Sarah. "My baby."

"Mom, what is up with you?"

"Where are those precious children?"

"Caitlin and Kyle? They're napping."

"Can I just peek in on them?"

"Peek in?" She ran her hand over her eyes. "What is going on?"

"Ryan told me." Her mother smiled widely. "I am so happy for you."

"Mother, I don't think you understand—"

"Oh, I know. It's a marriage of convenience. But a mother can hope for more can't she?"

She grabbed her mother's shoulders and looked into her eyes. "No. You can't hope. This isn't going to be a real marriage," she shouted.

"I'm home." Trent stood in the front door.

"Oh, Sarah," her mother breathed. "Is this the groom?"

She rolled her eyes. "Mother, Trent Kasey. Trent, my mother."

He crossed the room and took Catherine's hand in his, lifting it to his lips. Did he have to play so suave? Her mother would never forgive her when the marriage ended.

"Mrs. Goldwyne, it is a pleasure to meet you."

"Call me Catherine." Her mother giggled and flushed.

"Since you're home, Mom and I will get out of your hair." All she wanted was to escape from this embarrassing situation.

"There's no need. Why don't you ladies stay for dinner?" His gaze ran over the length of her. She felt her cheeks warm under his gaze.

"Actually, I came by to show Sarah something, and you aren't allowed to see it." Catherine's voice was a singsong.

It was probably some sinful negligee she'd never get the chance to wear. She already had one of those, chosen for her first wedding night that never happened.

"I'll see you tomorrow, Sarah." He lifted his hand to her cheek and ran the backs of his fingers over her jawline.

"Tomorrow." Her entire body burned from the simple touch. She had to get far away as quickly as possible.

"Sarah, you must bring Trent and the children for dinner tomorrow. Trent, we'll be expecting you," her mother called over her shoulder.

Chapter Nine

"I insist you wear this dress. It was my mother's. Then mine. I always wanted my daughter to wear it on the day she was married." Her mother laid the folds of white lace and satin out on Sarah's bed. "You're the only daughter I have."

"Mom, this is not a real marriage. I keep telling you that."

"Sarah Goldwyne, you might lie to yourself, but don't you try to lie to me. I saw the way you looked at that man. You're crazy about him."

Her mother's words hit a little too close to home. She couldn't allow herself to care about Trent that much. It would lead to certain heartache. She cared for him as a friend. As the father to Caitlin and Kyle, whom she loved dearly. That was all.

"Just think about the dress, Sarah. It would mean a lot to me. Since it's all so rushed, I won't get to attend the wedding. But it would be almost like being there if you'd wear the same dress I married your daddy in."

Not fair. The front door closed behind her mother with a firm click. She chewed on her lower lip. To wear the dress would be hypocritical. The marriage wasn't real. Not to wear the dress would break her mother's heart. What would it hurt to put on the folds of satin and detailed lacework? It was beautiful.

She ran her hands over the bodice. Tiny pearl beads formed a gentle pattern on the front panels. Cutout lace filled out the train. What would he think if she wore something like this to their wedding?

★ ★ ★ ★ ★

How exactly had she gotten trapped into taking Trent and the twins to Sunday dinner? Sometime between the time she'd left Trent's house and Sunday morning, her mother had managed to wring a promise from him that he would come to dinner.

"You don't have to do this," Sarah told Trent as she coaxed Nightfire into his cage in the back of the Explorer. He whined and held one paw up. "I know you don't like the cage, but you're safer. It's like a doggie car seat."

"Your mother was insistent. Since I'm marrying their daughter, your parents want to meet me."

"My mother is well aware that this isn't a real marriage. She's meddling." She slammed the door with enough force to cause Night to yelp. She grimaced. If there was one thing that drove her crazy, it was her mother.

"If you don't want us to come . . ." Trent trailed off.

Kyle reached his arms up, wanting Sarah to hold him. She picked him up. Her mother would drive him crazy with questions, but at least she'd have a few hours with the twins on a day she normally wouldn't get to see them.

"It's not your company I mind, it's the interrogation you're about to be put through that I don't like."

He laughed. "I can handle your mother."

She choked. "If you figure out how, let me and my brothers in on the secret, won't you? Let's move the car seats."

"I'll go get them." He whistled as he jogged to his Camaro.

She watched the sway of his hips. She whispered into Kyle's ear. "I could really fall for your uncle, if circumstances were different."

"Fwa. Fwa. Fwa." Kyle giggled.

Thank God it didn't even sound close to the actual word. All she needed was to let him know how attracted she was to him. He was cocky enough already.

"Here we go." He handed her the first car seat.

She opened one of the backseat doors and placed the car seat on the bench. The metal clasp to hold the seat belt in place gave her fits, as it always did. A fingernail snapped into the quick, and she jammed her finger into her mouth.

"Ouch."

"Let me see." He pulled her hand from her mouth and ran his thumb over the injured finger.

She could barely breathe around the sensations flooding her body. If he didn't stop . . .

"Looks painful." He dropped her hand.

She concentrated on staying upright. It wasn't fair for one man to be so full of sexual charisma. His grin was definitely mischievous as he leaned across her and adjusted the belt strap.

His shoulder brushed against her breasts, setting her on fire.

"One down, one to go." As he straightened his green gaze connected with hers, a knowing look in his eyes.

The rat. He knew exactly what he was doing to her. Well, she'd try to train a million Nightfires before she'd let him know he was just as hot as he apparently thought he was.

"Let's get moving. We don't want to be late. My mother will moan about it the entire day."

She ducked under his arm and grabbed the second car seat. Narrow escape. She'd just have to put this seat in without any help. She couldn't afford many close encounters like that one. Her heart was already hanging by a single thread. If it was pulled the least little bit, it was going to break.

★ ★ ★ ★ ★

If he didn't need her, he'd tell Sarah to forget the wedding. Why had she agreed to marry him anyway? The minute he got close enough to touch, she jumped away like a skittish puppy. Couldn't she feel the chemistry between them? He sure could, and it was getting harder and harder to keep his hands off her.

"I'll drive." He wanted something to take his mind off the fact that she'd be sitting a couple of feet away.

"It's my car." She jangled the keys.

"It's a male ego thing, Sarah." He held his hand out for the keys.

"On one condition."

"What is it with you and conditions?"

She raised one honey-colored brow, still holding the keys. He sighed.

"What?"

"The minute my mother mentions anything about our marriage, happily-ever-after, or grandchildren, you help me make an excuse to get out of there."

"Deal."

She dropped the keys into his outstretched palm. He considered grabbing her hand and pulling her into his arms for a slow kiss, but restrained himself at the last moment. He didn't want to rush her. Better to take things slow and easy.

She knew her family could be loud and boisterous. It was almost inevitable, with three brothers and a sports-fanatic father. She wondered what Trent thought of them. Not that it mattered. It wasn't as if he had to like them. Theirs wouldn't be a real marriage.

"Sarah, peel more potatoes. These are *men* you're

feeding, not little boys." Her mother raced around the kitchen yelling instructions.

"Could've fooled me," she muttered.

Trent chuckled. His gaze collided with Sarah's, and she felt the flush start at the base of her neck and rise into her cheeks. This had been a horrible idea. Her mother had already asked Trent at least twenty questions, and she apparently had no intention of stopping anytime soon.

"Trent, why don't you go watch TV with my father and brothers?"

"Trent wants to get to know me better, Sarah. Leave him alone." Her mother smiled and it reminded Sarah of the look a lion gave its prey just before attacking. "So, how old were you when your parents died?"

"Mother." She dropped the potato she was peeling. "I'm sure Trent doesn't want to discuss such personal issues—"

"Actually, I don't mind." He smiled wickedly, showing off his deep dimples. "After all, I'm marrying her daughter."

Caroline smiled at Trent. "Such a nice young man. I do hope Sarah can convince you to keep her."

Sarah's mouth dropped open. What could she possibly say? Honestly, she loved her mother, but there were times when she could absolutely never speak to the woman again because of her meddling.

"Close your mouth, dear. You'll catch flies."

"Hey, Sis." Matt looked into the bowl of potatoes she'd been peeling and slicing. "You need more. I'm a growing boy."

"If you keep eating enough for an army, the only way you'll be growing is out."

"I have the metabolism of a fifteen-year-old." Matt

patted his rock-hard stomach.

"And the maturity of one." She grinned at him.

"Who's the date?"

"Matt, this is Trent. Technically my fiancé."

"You think you're good enough for my sister?" Matt stared at him in a way that made it obvious he was sizing him up.

"I wouldn't attempt to say I was." Trent grinned.

She wanted to crawl into a dark corner and hide. Her family was the worst bunch of meddling—

"Sarah Belle." Ryan swung her into his arms and spun her around.

"Ryan. Where's Melody?"

"Her sister is visiting from Indiana. I'm supposed to meet back up with them later today. Is that Trent over there?"

"Yes," Trent said.

"I see you couldn't resist my sister's proposal."

She felt her cheeks heat again. What was wrong with these people? Surely she couldn't be from the same gene pool. She was adopted. That had to be it. Please let that be it.

"Best offer I've had in years."

"Sarah proposed?" Jeff stood in the doorway looking confused.

She groaned and pulled a dish towel over her head. "If I tap my heels three times, can I go home?"

"You can't go home until dinner is over." Her mother grabbed the towel off Sarah's head. "Now, peel more potatoes."

It was like an insane circus. Trent couldn't remember when he'd had more fun. True, some of the questions were personal, but they were all concerned about Sarah. He hoped she realized how lucky she was to have so many people who cared about her. He missed that more than he cared to admit.

"Pass more potatoes." Ryan stared at the empty bowl where the potatoes had been.

She glared at him.

He covered his laughter behind a fake cough.

"I'll take some more, too," Jeff added.

"I told you to peel more potatoes, Sarah." Sarah's mother clicked her tongue.

"I wish there were more potatoes," added Matt.

"Oh, shut up." She glared at all three of her brothers.

He couldn't help noticing the way her pupils dilated the tiniest bit when she was angry. He wondered if they'd look the same way after a satisfying night of lovemaking.

"Kyle and Caitlin, are you finished?" he asked them.

"Grandma has some cake for them." Sarah's mother rushed to the kitchen.

He frowned. He wasn't sure he liked the idea of the kids thinking of Sarah's parents as Grandma and Grandpa, it would lead to heartache if they got too attached.

Caroline returned with rich brown chocolate cake.

"It's been so long since this house was filled children." Caroline sighed wistfully. "I've wanted grandchildren for ages."

A sharp painful kick landed on his shin. She stared at him and made motions with her eyes. Time to go? He grinned evilly.

She cleared her throat.

He sat back and crossed his arms, maintaining eye contact.

"Of course Ryan managed to put the cart before the

horse, but Sarah is the one I really want to see settled."

She coughed.

"Sarah, what is the matter with you?" her mother demanded.

Sarah's face turned rosy.

Okay, she'd suffered long enough. He pushed his chair back.

"Mrs. Goldwyne, thank you for a wonderful meal, but I'm afraid I have to get the twins home."

"So early?" Caroline's lips turned down.

"I'm afraid so."

"Well, I suppose we'll have more opportunities to visit."

Not if Sarah had her way, Trent suspected.

Sarah hadn't spoken a word since they'd left her parents. Trent reached over and laid his hand on hers.

"It wasn't so bad."

"You must think my family is horrible." She looked out the passenger window.

"I think they love you."

"They do. Sometimes I feel so smothered though. Any boy who ever tried to date me had to make it past my mother and then all three of my brothers. Needless to say, not many tried."

He chuckled. "I guess I should thank your brothers that you're still available, then."

"If only their good judgment had held out." She crossed her arms and shivered, a faraway look in her eyes.

What did she mean by that? Had some man hurt her? That would explain her reluctance to get involved.

"Sarah, are you sure about this marriage?" As much as he needed her help, he didn't want to force her into a situation she would regret.

"Of course. I can't let that horrid man get those two precious babies." She turned to look in the backseat. "They're asleep."

"You've been good for them, Sarah. They've missed having a woman in their lives." *Not that she or anyone could ever replace Melissa,* he reminded himself.

"I love having them in my life," she whispered.

"I'm worried how they'll handle both of us leaving for Vegas." *Will they think I've disappeared from their lives the way their mother did?*

"My brother is great with kids. Last year, he took six of my cousins on a camping trip. They all got poison ivy . . ."

"What?"

"They'll be fine, Trent. Relax."

He took a deep breath and let it out. "You're right."

"As usual." She grinned. "Let's get the rugrats and my dog home."

Home. After Thursday *home* would mean the same house. Their home.

Chapter Ten

At 7:45 on Thursday morning, Sarah arrived with Ryan and a diminutive blonde in tow. Trent was trying to wipe crayon marks off the once-white living room wall.

"Trent, this is Ryan's fiancée—Melody." Sarah's lips twitched at the purple swirls Trent was trying to scrub into oblivion.

"We can get those crayon marks. A little diluted ammonia takes them right off. My brothers liked to mark on the walls when they were kids." Ryan's smile was wide.

"Ryan, you're forgetting, it was *you* who enjoyed coloring on the walls. I would think you'd still have a tanned hide to prove it."

He watched the gentle play between brother and sister with a lump in his throat. God but he missed Melissa. Sometimes, he could almost forget for a while, but then the twins would look at him with a certain expression or a word would remind him of her, and it'd strike out at him with the force of a wrecking ball.

He tossed the rag onto the coffee table and grabbed his suitcase, almost losing his grip on it his palms were so moist.

Ryan stepped close, almost nose to nose with Trent, the smile gone. "Just one thing. Hurt my sister, and I hurt you. *Capisce?*"

She laughed and pulled Ryan back. "He's kidding, Trent. He watches too much TV, just like Dad. Did you tell the twins good-bye?"

He nodded, unable to speak. Since their mother had died, he'd never been apart from them overnight. What if

Caitlin had one of her bad dreams? What if Kyle woke up and needed one of their special Dino the Dinosaur stories to go back to sleep? Sarah's brother wouldn't know who Dino was since the dinosaur was a figment of Trent's imagination.

"They'll be fine. Ryan is great with kids." She squeezed his arm reassuringly.

He swallowed and nodded once. It wasn't as if he had a choice. If he wanted to keep the children out of Winters's greedy grasp, he had to marry Sarah. They were running short on time.

"Let's do it then." He thanked Ryan again and walked out the front door. She frowned but followed him to the car. She was silent until they pulled off Viewpoint and onto the main road.

"Is that how you think of marriage? As some horrible *it* that you have to suffer through to achieve your goal?"

That was exactly how he thought of it, Trent realized. But he couldn't very well tell Sarah that. She could still choose not to go through with the whole crazy charade, and then where would he be?

He shrugged. "Let's just say the examples I've seen haven't been the Brady Bunch."

"My family was." She turned in her seat to face him.

"Mine wasn't. My parents were about the closest I've seen and look what happened to that family. Then, the one time I tried to marry someone, she decided she'd rather be dead."

He reached for the dial on the radio, but Sarah stopped him with a hand on his arm.

"Your fiancée killed herself?" Her eyes were filled with a sympathy he didn't want.

"It was a long time ago."

"How horrible for you."

He shrugged.

"Don't you want a family someday? Children of your own?"

"I already have both."

She let go of his arm. "Music would be nice." She seemed relaxed, as if a weight had been lifted from her shoulders.

Had she been scared he'd expect more from their marriage than a temporary arrangement? Perhaps she'd been frightened he'd want forever. He frowned. It didn't sit well that the thought of forever with him was so unsettling for her.

Sarah wasn't sure when it had happened, but she suspected she cared a lot more about Trent Kasey than she'd anticipated. Perhaps it was the first time she'd seen him hug Kyle as though the child were more precious than gold. Or maybe it was the patient strokes as he tried to erase the crayon marks from a morning of busy toddlerhood. Whatever the reason, a feeling of familiarity and warmth flooded through her veins, warming her.

It was a feeling she'd never experienced with Paul, the man she'd thought she loved with a pureness. The man she'd wanted to marry and spend her life with. Or had that been Paul's idea? Paul had always tried to mold her to suit his needs, she realized with the sudden clarity of time.

With Trent, she could be herself. He had no unrealistic expectations about what she should be. Paul had always insisted she dress a certain way, talk a certain way; he'd even commented on her laugh once, saying it was too robust for a woman. He'd asked her to laugh in a tinkly way, whatever that meant.

But if what she'd felt with Paul had truly been so shallow as to not compare to this, how could she possibly put a name to her budding emotions? She wanted to keep the twins away from Winters and be a mother to them, but there was another reason she'd asked him to marry her. Even had he not had Caitlin and Kyle, she would have wanted to be his wife. His need had given her an excuse to seek what she wanted.

Of course if he didn't have the twins, if he wanted children of his own, the situation would have been impossible. But, because of a strange twist of fate, it no longer seemed insurmountable. When he'd said he didn't want his own children, Sarah felt as light as the foam of a crashing wave.

Perhaps she could convince him to give their marriage a real chance. To give her a chance. What if it was possible for them to fall in love? Her top teeth landed on her bottom lip, a habit she was trying to break but always returned to when worried. She didn't know how it would all work out in the end; she only knew that she had to give it her best shot. If she was to allow herself to love again, this was the time. Trent was the man. At the moment, she couldn't imagine loving someone else, didn't even remember there was anyone else in the world but this man, this moment, the next heartbeat of time.

He pulled into the long-term parking lot at the airport. "What time does the plane leave?"

"In an hour."

His dark head whipped around so quickly, Sarah winced at the threatened whiplash. "What?"

"We'll need to run." She smiled. "Let's hope the lines aren't too long. We'll just check all our baggage."

He grabbed their bags, locked the car, and, taking her hand, ran for the airport shuttle.

"Why would you cut it so close?" he panted.

"Why would you?"

"Touché."

The shuttle door slid closed behind them with a gentle hydraulic hiss. She collapsed into the nearest seat and Trent slid in next to her. She tried to ignore the volcanic heat of his thigh pressed against hers.

"I'm curious about something." She pushed a loose strand of hair out of her face.

He groaned low in his throat. She ignored him.

"Why did the lady say no?"

Blank green eyes stared at her. He had no clue what she was talking about. Maybe she should slow down. Catch her breath. Was she so short-winded because of the sprint to catch the bus or because he was near?

"The lady you asked to marry you. You said she had other plans."

"I didn't ask her." His voice was like black velvet sliding sensuously over her heated skin.

"Why not?"

"There was this red truck in her driveway all weekend, and I thought it might be a romantic interest in her life. Turns out it was her brother."

What did joy feel like? If it felt like tiny bursts of champagne bubbles floating through your veins, then that was what she felt.

"I was the woman you were going to ask?"

He nodded.

She punched him on the arm. "You made me propose, make a fool out of myself, and you were planning to ask me all along?"

"There's nothing foolish about you, Sarah." The warmth that poured out of his gaze heated her from the outside in.

She took a deep breath. If she had any hope of turning

this into a real marriage, and that was something she wanted more with each passing moment, she had to be honest. Any secrets would only come back to bite her later.

"Trent, I have to tell you something before we get married."

"You're ill." His eyes looked worried.

"No."

"Already married." Now those green orbs were twinkling with mischief.

"No."

"You don't like men?"

"No!"

"You're pregnant. I thought it was odd how you made peanut butter and maple syrup sandwiches the other day."

She swallowed. "That could only be further from the truth if you drove it to the South Pole."

He must have sensed the depth of her overflowing emotions, because he took her hand between both of his and rubbed the suddenly chilled skin gently, warming it where his skin touched hers.

"I'm not pregnant, and I'll never be pregnant."

"Sarah, if you want children, I'm sure some man out there . . ."

"Just listen, Trent." God, why did this have to be so hard? How many times had she gone over this conversation in her mind and imagined the man she loved turning his back on her once again because she couldn't fulfill his future plans? She could love Trent so easily. Maybe it was better that he turn his back now, while she could still hold back her emotions. If she wasn't already in love.

"Three years ago I was pregnant. I lost the baby in an . . . umm . . . accident. I can't have children now. Ever."

She wanted to turn away. To crawl under the shuttle

seats and hide from the condemnation she knew would be in his eyes. Now he would say he couldn't go through with it. He'd take his chances with the courts. Then he'd turn and walk away.

Reluctantly, she raised her gaze to his face. His gentle, handsome face was so filled with compassion, understanding, and acceptance that it took her breath away. Without saying a word, he reached over and took her in his arms, gently stroking her back the way he might if Caitlin or Kyle needed comforting.

Sarah's world rocked. Every reality she'd known since Paul had walked out on her was challenged and broken into a million insane pieces. The ice that had numbed her heart and protected it from the death Paul had tried to deal it melted into a pool of emotions that sucked her breath away.

She took a shaky breath. She had thought in the car that she might be able to learn to love this man. Now she knew that love wasn't something you learned. It was something that was. Love didn't always come with a gentle awakening after years of knowing someone, but it could sometimes strike you down as swiftly as a well-aimed arrow from a crafty Greek god with wings.

She loved Trent. Loved him and would build a life with him for as long as he would have her. If it was three weeks, three years, or three lifetimes, she would grasp whatever time she was granted and try to savor each memory. They might have to last her three lifetimes if she failed to make him see how wonderful their marriage could be.

"Sarah." That was all he said. Just her name.

She couldn't have spoken in that moment, even if he'd expected it of her. Her throat was so clogged with emotion, she would surely have gone into an insane coughing fit until she passed out, and wouldn't that have been a fine way to start off this new phase of their relationship?

"Delta. Northwest . . ." The bus driver rattled off several names, and it took Sarah a moment to realize he'd named their airline.

"That's us." He jumped to his feet and grabbed the bags. "Hurry."

After the lift she'd felt from his understanding, Sarah felt a swift letdown as he shifted from their embrace to panic-we-have-to-catch-the-plane-mode. *There will be plenty of time to talk later,* she told herself. Once they were on the plane, he wouldn't be able to escape her as easily. She smiled and raced after him.

Trent couldn't run fast enough, and not just because he had a plane to catch. The emotions that had swirled through him as he'd held Sarah's fragile shaking body against his had touched some deep core he'd hidden away for a long time and not allowed anyone new to touch.

He couldn't allow himself to care. To care was to lose. He already loved the twins. It wasn't an emotion you could turn off. It was very possible he would lose them both, even with his marriage to Sarah. Fifty-fifty odds, Gregg had said. Much less than he would have liked.

He just didn't have room in his life to care about anyone else. To worry about them. To grow alarmed every time they were fifteen minutes late and he heard about a car accident. Every person he'd ever loved he'd lost, so it was smart to limit the people he loved. First his mother and father in a car accident. Donna by her own hand. Then Melissa. Who would be next? He didn't think he could bear it again. He didn't want to find out.

They checked their luggage at the counter, waited through a long line at the security check point, and slid onto the plane just as the flight attendant was shutting the door. Every bright orange seat contained a passenger, except for two lone seats. Three rows apart from one another. Normally, the plane would be half empty. Just his luck.

"Separate seats?" he asked.

She shrugged, turning sideways and stepping past the stewardess who was running around distributing pillows. Three rows back, a young mother tried to console a screaming baby.

"It was last-minute. We're lucky we got on at all."

Lucky wasn't the word he would have used. It would be too easy to care about Sarah. To want to keep her in his life forever. He had to keep in mind that this was a temporary arrangement until the twins' future could be secured. Then Sarah would head back to her safe little world of walks on the beach with her dog, and he would resume raising Caitlin and Kyle and trying not to botch things up too badly.

"I'll take the screaming-baby seat." She headed for the row just behind the wings and helped the mother secure a pink-striped diaper bag under the seat in front of her.

Trent watched as she smiled at the baby and tried to distract it from its insistent crying. The mother, bouncing the child on her knee, smiled gratefully at Sarah. Hot emotion burned his throat and made his eyes sting.

He sat in the hideous orange seat and tried to drown his thoughts in the flight magazine in front of him. But a story about Vermont's covered bridges failed to hold his interest.

Too many thoughts were swirling too quickly through his mind. They should have signed an agreement. Should have discussed more details about the marriage. There hadn't been time for them to get to know each other well enough to take this step, even temporarily, and he suspected there were a lot more layers to Sarah Goldwyne yet to be uncovered.

Chapter Eleven

"Mother! What are you doing here?" Sarah's mother stood guard in the hotel lobby.

"I wasn't about to miss my only daughter's wedding." Catherine raised a handkerchief to her eye and dabbed. "Let's get you upstairs and get you into that wedding dress. I'm only here for a few hours; then we have to catch an evening flight back to California."

"Is Daddy here?"

"He's in the bar, watching TV." Her mother frowned.

She hid her grin. Daddy and that television. She spotted Jeff and Matt at the check-in desk talking to a pretty blond clerk.

"My sister just might need a bridesmaid." Jeff leaned his elbows on the desk and moved closer to the blonde. "You interested in the job?"

"I have a job." The blonde ignored her brothers and typed rapidly on a computer keyboard.

Her father wandered out of the hotel bar and stopped in front of her.

"I'm here to walk you down the aisle." Her father kissed her on the cheek.

"Thanks, Daddy. This isn't a real marriage, though. You didn't have to come."

"Baby girl, I'm here for you through real, fake, and in-between. Not even the Super Bowl would keep me away." Her father patted her awkwardly on the shoulder.

The ceremony was surprisingly short and too official-sounding. The justice of the peace spoke the words as though he were quoting the Ten Commandments and looked at them sternly over wire-rimmed spectacles as they repeated their vows.

Sarah's face had gone from pale to pasty. Her wide blue eyes looked terrified, and she was so tense he wouldn't have been surprised to see her sprint from the grounds of the Tropicana.

"Beautiful," Catherine whispered, lifting the handkerchief to her eye again.

Marriage meant more to Sarah than she'd led him to believe. That was obvious from the lacy dress she wore and her reaction to the ceremony. He didn't want to admit it, but the words were having a strange effect on him, too. He felt as though they were a real couple making a promise to love, honor, and cherish.

"Do you, Sarah Goldwyne, take Trent Kasey to love, honor, and obey?" The judge glared at them again over his spectacles as if daring them to break the vows he uttered.

She swallowed and rubbed the toe of her white pump against the jackpot red outdoor carpeting that covered the smooth concrete floor. Was she having second thoughts? If she backed out now, there was no way he could find someone else to marry before the hearing. He didn't want to marry anyone else!

"I will love, honor, and cherish, Your Honor, but I'm not sure I can keep the vow to obey."

The man's thin lips twitched as though tempted to lift in a smile. "Obey is traditional, and this young man doesn't look as though he would abuse the vow."

She lifted her chin, and he realized something else about this multifaceted woman he was marrying. She was stubborn.

"I promise not to make you rub my feet more than once a day," he whispered.

She smiled at him but shook her head. "Please change the vow to cherish. That I can do."

Did she mean that? He didn't want to be cherished. He just wanted to get this ceremony over with, get through the social worker's visit, the hearing after that, and then get on with his life.

The man repeated the vow as Sarah had requested. She smiled at him, and it was like the sun coming out from behind a heavy rain cloud.

"In that case, I do."

He chuckled. When the judge pronounced them husband and wife, Trent sighed with relief. Until his next words . . .

"You may now kiss the bride."

Sarah's mouth shaped into a perfect circle of surprise. He hadn't expected or planned for the intimacy of a kiss. Not that he was going to pass up the opportunity. He'd wanted to kiss her since her dog had knocked him down and he'd looked up the longest pair of legs he'd ever seen and into her blue eyes.

"Sarah." He gently grasped her upper arms and pulled her into a loose embrace.

She sighed and leaned into him, tilting her head up for his descending lips.

"Kiss me," she whispered. "Everyone is watching."

Trent's muscles tightened like coiled springs. The sweet scent of her invaded his senses. His lips claimed hers under the watchful gaze of the onlookers.

Her arms slid around his waist, her firm warm breasts pressing into his chest and increasing his heart rate. Sarah's lips parted on a soft sigh, and he deepened the kiss, claiming the honeyed recesses of her mouth.

He didn't want the kiss to end and reality to take over. The sound of applause and one or two catcalls from Matt and Jeff invaded the mystical spell that Trent and Sarah had both fallen under, and Trent pulled back from Sarah. The flash of a camera nearly blinded him. She stared at him with those wide, innocent blue eyes, and smiled. "I don't think I've ever received applause for a kiss before."

"If ever a kiss warranted it . . ." He wanted to haul her back into his arms. Instead, he had to paste a smile on his face and endure a long after-wedding dinner. Sarah's mother pulled out a round cake with tiny, pink sugar bells on it.

"I know it isn't much, but it was last-minute." Sarah's mother had tears in her eyes.

"It's a beautiful cake," he said.

"Thanks, Mom." Sarah hugged her mother.

They cut the cake, drank a few sips of champagne, and endured several pictures Mrs. Goldwyne insisted on taking for her scrapbook. After a torturous hour, the Goldwynes announced they had a plane to catch, and everyone hugged them and wished them well.

They walked the family to their taxicab, then Trent took Sarah's elbow and guided her toward the bank of elevators on the far wall of the lobby. She didn't speak again until the elevator doors slid shut behind them. "Do you think we could try that kiss again sometime?" Her hands were clasped in front of her, and a few stray curls had escaped from her upswept hair.

He groaned. God help him, temporary or not, the only thing he could think of was making her his wife in the most biblical way. If he didn't get out of this elevator and to a public place, he was going to hit the red panic button and make love to her right here against the mirrored wall of the elevator.

Instead, he jabbed the button to return to the main lobby.

"Where are we going?"

"Shopping. We need wedding bands."

"Oh." She sighed. "Do you think I could go change clothes first? This dress is a family heirloom."

He wondered if she seemed disappointed? He needed to set some ground rules to this arrangement. They'd married so quickly that they hadn't had time to discuss the terms of their marriage.

"I'll wait for you in the lounge." He paused. "Since this is a temporary arrangement, I think it might be best if I slept on the couch tonight."

She swallowed and blinked a couple of times. "Of course, Trent."

But as she turned away, tears glittered on her cheeks. *I didn't mean to hurt her feelings. Why can't I be smooth and suave?*

She didn't want a wedding band. It made the whole thing seem too real, and Trent had just made it clear that he saw their marriage as temporary. While she'd been entertaining fantasies of happily-ever-after, he'd been figuring out how they could sleep in the same room and not become involved.

At what point did hope die? Was it in the still quiet hours of the morning, when the silence pushed in like suffocating folds of black velvet? No, hope hadn't died then, or she would never have agreed to marry Trent. It seemed as though her entire adult life had been spent in pursuit of an unattainable goal. Now, that goal was close enough to appear as a shimmering mirage, but when she reached out to capture it, it sifted through her fingers like the dry sand of the desert.

He led her to a jewelry store in the shopping mall of Caesar's Palace, nestled under a constantly changing ceiling depicting a sunny day turning slowly to midnight and back again.

"Let's try on this one." He pointed to a simple wedding set with a teardrop-shaped diamond and matching wedding band.

Sarah's hand trembled as she held out her fingers, and he slipped the ring in place.

"What do you think, Sarah?" His green eyes were shaded with gold flecks. It was impossible to tell what he was thinking.

She looked down at the rings resting on her finger as if they'd always belonged there. The diamond engagement ring was cut with a clarity that reminded Sarah of a fine crystal prism. She turned her hand from side to side, the diamond catching the reflection of the overhead lights and throwing it back in all directions.

The ring had to cost a fortune. She couldn't let Trent spend this kind of money on a temporary marriage. She'd just have to return the ring when they separated anyway. Her throat burning, Sarah took the ring off and handed it back to the salesman.

"Just a plain gold band will do." She forced herself to turn from the ring and study the case with gold wedding bands.

"You didn't like the ring?" his voice whispered against the back of her neck.

She took a deep breath, imagining what it would feel like to have his warm lips touch her there.

"The ring is beautiful, but hardly practical in our situation."

She turned and met his gaze. A flicker of male pride stabbed through the green depths of his eyes before he nodded once and asked the salesman to show them matching gold bands.

No diamonds marred the wheat-colored ring Trent handed her. She tried it on for size and found that it fit well enough for their short-lived marriage.

"This one works." She pretended to be interested in the watch display in the center of the store, hiding the tears that threatened to surface. Normally, she wasn't so prone to tears, but this was her wedding day, so she was entitled, whether it was a real marriage or not.

"Ready?" He wore the matching gold band to hers, and Sarah's stomach slammed itself into a hard knot of pain. If only . . . There was no point in "if onlying." She had one shot at this marriage, and she would grasp it with every bit of strength in her until it faded out of reach.

"Let's see the sights," she suggested, wrapping her arm companionably in his.

Trent's dark brows arched, but he walked alongside her.

Outside, the day had faded to dusk, but the night was lit brightly from the hotel signs and flashing advertisements. Heat from the hundred-degree day still rose from the sidewalk and enveloped their ankles, but the air at her shoulders felt slightly chilled.

She took a deep breath of the dry air. "God, I love this town."

He laughed. "Don't tell me I've married a gambler."

"Lead me to the slot machines."

"It's your wedding night, m'lady. As you request."

She wondered what his reaction would be if she requested he take her back to their room and make wild, passionate love to her? It was her wedding night after all. She suspected such a bold move on her part would only drive him emotionally further from her than ever. There was already a chasm as large as the Grand Canyon separating them.

He was civil, but it was as if a part of him was walled off from her. He had set up certain barriers that she couldn't break through. They were stronger than plaster or brick, which she could have torn down, even if it was piece by piece. These barriers went much deeper and, she suspected, were built on past pain.

He had to admit, it wasn't exactly what he had envisioned for his wedding night. But he was relieved Sarah wanted to hit the casinos and not return straight to their room. How was he going to keep his hands off her? He couldn't become intimate with her when she was planning on leaving after the custody was determined.

Part of him wanted to take her to bed, love her with every pent-up ounce of passion in his body, and keep her by his side forever. He couldn't cross that threshold. Once he did, there would be no holding back the feelings he was restraining by a single thread of self-control.

"Did you see that?" She glared at her machine. "It acted like it was going to hit the jackpot, then slid past at the last second."

He chuckled as he added another three hundred quarters to his stockpile. She glanced at the digital readout of his total.

"Care to share some of those quarters?" She batted her lashes flirtatiously.

"No way. You lost all of yours already."

"Let's go play something else. I've always wanted to try my hand at the craps tables." The sparkle of excitement in her eyes was contagious.

"Okay, but you still aren't getting my quarters." He cashed the machine out and followed her to the noisiest table in the casino.

She bounced onto her tiptoes to watch the action. "Isn't this fun? How do we play?"

He rolled his eyes. She picked one of the worst odds games in the casino and didn't even know how to play.

"You either wait for a turn to throw the dice or you bet on the guy throwing." He nodded as a balding man of about fifty threw the dice against the shallow wall of the craps pit. "Like that."

"I'll wait to throw," she decided.

When the table opened up, Sarah placed her bet and then slung the dice. While she waited for the dice to roll to a standstill, her hip brushed against the apex of his thighs. Trent's body was instantly aroused.

The crush of people surrounding them shouted as the dice spun to a stop.

"Did I win?"

"You sure did, honey." He placed an arm around her shoulders.

She jumped up and down in excitement, scooped up her chips, and headed for the cashier's booth.

"Hey! Where are you going?" he asked.

"I'm quitting while I'm ahead."

He laughed. "You're not ahead if you count what you lost in the slots."

She leaned over and whispered conspiratorially. "I know, but I'd rather quit now than wait until I've lost all my money."

He watched her cute little rear in the tight red skirt as she swayed up to the window. Had she worn that outfit on purpose to provoke him? He bit hard on the inside of his cheeks. Delaying the return to their room hadn't helped one bit. If anything, he was in worse shape now than he'd been after the wedding. How was he going to hide his arousal from her? The lady crawled behind the strongest defenses he could erect and ripped them down from the inside out.

Chapter Twelve

They returned to the hotel in silence. The air was heavy with suppressed tension that had shock pulses dancing over Trent's skin. It wasn't until they were in the room that Sarah spoke.

"Let's order champagne and strawberries."

If she had told him she was from another planet, he wouldn't have been more surprised. "You're hungry?"

"No. But I always thought I'd have champagne and strawberries on my wedding night." Her eyes took on a hazy glow, and she looked as though she were somewhere else. Suddenly, Sarah looked very young and very vulnerable. A clutch of protectiveness centered in his chest. The last thing either of them needed was an emotional attachment. This marriage couldn't last. Wasn't meant to last. It wasn't permanent. Why couldn't his body understand that?

"Maybe you should wait, Sarah."

"For what, Trent?" Her laugh was as bitter as lemon rinds. "The love of my life? The man who promised to be there forever one hot, hazy night on the beach? The same one who dumped me when our baby died, and he learned I couldn't give him the children he wanted? I'm tired of waiting."

Her pain was a living, breathing force that filled the air in the room and throbbed around them. He wanted to wipe it away, take it on himself, and get his hands on the bastard who had hurt her.

All he could do was pull her into his arms and stroke his fingers over her hair, much like he'd comfort Caitlin or Kyle. Except this was a grown-up woman in his arms, and his body recognized that fact. Her breasts pressed softly against his chest until his heartbeat thundered in his ears.

He brushed a soft kiss across her forehead. "I'll order the champagne, Sarah. You deserve the wedding night of your dreams."

Her smile was a little shaky, but it was a smile that warmed him. "Thank you, Trent."

The words hung in the air between them as if they meant so much more than what their ancestors had intended that they mean. *This* thank you sounded more like a caress. A meeting of souls.

"I think I'll take a bath while you call room service."

He watched until the bathroom door closed behind her, wondering how he was going to keep his libido under control while his mind imagined her soft skin sliding underneath warm sudsy bubbles. He groaned.

Twenty minutes later, Sarah emerged from the bathroom with rosy cheeks, looking a little more cheerful. He tried to ignore the seductive scent that trailed her into the room. When had he lost control of the situation?

She lifted the metal lid covering the bowl of strawberries. "Hmmmm . . ." She lifted one bright red piece of the fruit and held it up to her lips.

Trent's mouth went dry as she bit into the soft flesh and closed her eyes in ecstasy. *God, doesn't she realize what she is doing to me?* But when she opened her eyes, and he saw the amusement shimmering in their blue depths, he was fairly certain she knew exactly what effect she was having on him.

"Champagne?" He'd already uncorked the bottle, and now he held it up for her inspection.

She lifted one of the finely etched crystal flutes from the serving tray and held it out to him. "Fill her to the rim. It's my wedding night."

He filled it halfway. They both needed to be fully in control of their senses if they were going to resist the shimmering heat growing between them. Whether he wanted to resist or not.

She grabbed the bowl of fruit and sat down on the sofa. She patted the spot next to her. "Sit."

"Sarah, I'm not sure . . ."

"Oh, just sit. I know you don't want a real marriage, but we can be friends, can't we?"

Friends? The last thing he wanted was to be friends. He wanted much more from Sarah at this moment, but knew it wasn't fair to either of them to start a relationship that couldn't last.

Her lashes fluttered down onto her cheeks in a move that signaled her hurt and pain. The last thing he wanted was to cause her any more torment. He moved next to her and sat down.

"Hungry?" She held a strawberry up to his mouth.

He shook his head no. She'd stolen the breath from his body, and he couldn't even talk. Sarah shrugged and brought the strawberry to her own lips, sucking on it softly before taking a bite.

"Let's talk about the court investigator's visit." She took a sip of champagne, and Trent's gaze fell to where her lips lingered against the delicate glass. It took a moment before her words made sense to him.

"She's coming next week."

"I mean our story, silly. We need to have our story straight."

She scooted closer, and Trent, God help him, welcomed her warm thigh pressing against his.

She plucked another strawberry from the dish, and his

body tightened even more. If he survived until then, she was right, they needed to be prepared to answer some difficult questions.

"So, are we in love?"

Trent's head snapped up, and he met her amused blue eyes.

"For the social worker, silly." Another crisp bite of the strawberry.

"L-love." He stuttered. He jumped to his feet. *I never stutter. What is she doing to me?*

"What's wrong, Trent?"

"I'm tired, Sarah. We can talk about this tomorrow."

Her smile disappeared. "Of course. I wouldn't want to keep you from your sleep."

He ignored the downward pull of her lips. He knew she was disappointed. Could feel hurt and bewilderment arching out from her in shimmering waves of emotion. But she was reining it in tightly; it showed in the rigid set of her slim shoulders and the angle of her chin.

"I'll sleep on the couch," he reminded her.

She set the bowl of strawberries on the low table next to her abandoned champagne. He regretted spoiling her enjoyment in the decadent meal, but he was the wrong man for her to share it with. Certainly, there was someone out there who would love Sarah and give her the wedding night of her dreams. He just wasn't that man. *I just can't let myself love anyone else,* he shouted in his head. *Never again.*

It was midnight when Sarah sat straight up in the huge, lonely bed, awakened by her own screams. Her hair was tangled around her, and the sheets had shifted down and trapped her ankles.

She fumbled for a light switch, needing the brightness to

chase away the lingering shadows of devastation. Before she could find the switch for the bedside lamp, the bright overhead glare of the ceiling light filled the room.

"Sarah?" Trent's hair was mussed.

"I'm sorry if I woke you, Trent. Go back to sleep." Her voice came out husky and a little breathless. She was still struggling to gain her composure after the dream. A dream she had over and over. A dream she would give anything to shake out of her life.

"Are you okay?" A dark shadow stubbled his jaw, and Sarah studied him for a moment, deciding she liked the roguish look on him.

"I'm fine." She fumbled for the tangled sheets, intending to cover her sheer nightgown. She'd chosen it for her first wedding night, the one that never happened. It was only fitting that she wear it for this wedding night, the one that almost happened. A mirthless chuckle escaped, only to end in a hiccup.

He crossed the room in three powerful strides, sat on the edge of the bed, and pulled her into his arms. She wanted to push him away, but he felt so genuine. For a moment she closed her eyes and indulged in a fantasy. If only their marriage were real, and Trent loved her.

"Bad dream?" His breath stirred the hair on top of her head.

"A recurring one."

"Want to talk about it?"

"Not really."

He pulled back and frowned at her. "How do you expect to get over it, if you don't talk about it?"

"Who do you tell your dreams to, Trent?" She shot back, on the defensive.

He shrugged.

"That's what I thought."

"Maybe, if I had someone to tell them to, it would help." His voice stroked over her, soft as satin pillowcases.

"You have me." Had she really said that? She wanted to kick herself.

He cupped the palm of his hand over her shoulder. In her life, there had only been two things she'd really wanted. The first had been a child. The other was sitting right in front of her. So close and yet so far out of her reach it made her heart ache with longing. If they were to have the smallest chance, that long shot that she could make him care, make their marriage real, one of them was going to have to open up. She had to make the first move. Trust him.

"Paul—he . . ." The words choked off as bands of pain tightened around her throat.

He fluffed the pillows behind her and laid her gently back against them. She wanted to cry out as she left his embrace, but he was right with her, stretching out on his side and propping his head up.

"Take your time." His eyes gleamed warm green.

"I don't know where to start." A single tear escaped and trailed a blazing path down her cheek.

He reached out and caught it on the tip of his finger. "Start with the dream, Sarah."

"Paul is driving too fast. Too reckless. We run into an embankment. Then I can hear my baby crying, and I search for it. But the faster I run, the fainter the cries grow, and I know I'll never be able to save him."

He brushed a loose strand of hair off her forehead. His tenderness touched Sarah in the deepest part of her soul. Why did he have to be so perfect, so wonderful, and so determined not to fall in love?

"You lost your baby in a car accident?"

"Paul had been drinking. We ran off the road. They had to cut me out of the wreckage. The baby died inside of me; they induced labor, and he was stillborn at five months."

Sarah's voice caught, and she bit her lip. He pulled her against him, laying her head on his firm shoulder. She took a deep breath, taking on his strength as her own to continue the story.

"P-Paul . . ." She had to stop as the pain overwhelmed her. "He forced me to get in the car that night. I knew he'd been drinking. He just grabbed me by the arm and pushed me in. He scared me, and I thought that if I just went along, he wouldn't hurt the baby." Her laugh was bitter.

"Sarah, you couldn't have known." His lips caressed her forehead.

She closed her eyes, savoring the vague citrus of his aftershave. Moments like this needed to be frozen, imprinted on her soul for the dark lonely years facing her when Trent wouldn't be in her life.

"Tell me the rest, Sarah. You need to get it out."

"When the doctors said I might not ever be able to carry another baby because of the internal injuries from the accident . . ." She didn't want to tell Trent this. What man wouldn't feel the same way Paul had? How would she ever recover if Trent turned coldly from her? Fear lengthened her silence.

"Sarah, trust me." His voice rumbled low in his chest, soothing her.

"Paul said I wasn't a woman any longer, and the engagement was off. He walked out of my life that day and never looked back. He never called to make sure I recovered. Never asked about me to my knowledge. It was as if I had died in that car accident as far as he was concerned."

He was silent for so long that Sarah began to shake nervously. Could he feel the tremors wracking her body? God, what was he thinking? Was he trying to think of a gentle way to tell her he felt the same way? He wouldn't be as cruel as Paul had been, that wasn't in Trent's nature, but it would hurt a thousand times more than Paul's betrayal.

"And you believed what he told you?" He still held her in his arms.

She wondered if that was a good sign.

"How could I expect a man to give up having his own children for me?"

"Don't you realize that if a man truly loved you, it wouldn't make a difference?"

His words shocked Sarah down to the tips of her toes. Of all the reactions she'd expected, it hadn't been that. If a man truly loved her . . . If only Trent was that man.

"There are so many children out there who need good homes, Sarah. If a man truly loved you but wanted children, don't you think he'd realize that?"

"But what if he wanted his own children?"

"What difference does it make? Are you telling me you'd really want to marry a man who couldn't love a child that wasn't from his seed? Such a man would be very narrow-minded, and I can't imagine you loving him, Sarah."

"Trent Kasey, you are very special." She couldn't help it. She had to kiss him.

His grin was slightly lopsided when she pulled back. "You're pretty special yourself, Sarah Kasey. Now can we please get some sleep?" He hit the switch to dim the overhead lights and pulled her snugly to him.

She lay stiffly for a few moments. He planned to stay in bed with her? Apparently. He also quite obviously only intended to sleep. She sighed and snuggled closer. It was a step forward. She could live with that.

Chapter Thirteen

"Do you think the twins will be okay with me living in the house?" She clutched her purse nervously in her damp palms.

She'd been asking questions for the last fifteen minutes, firing them off as quickly as Trent could answer them.

"They love you, Sarah." He reached over and squeezed her clenched fists. "They're used to having you around."

"When is the court investigator coming again?"

"Friday at noon." Amazingly, his voice sounded calm.

"What do we tell her? Our marriage was so sudden. What if she's suspicious?"

"We tell her you couldn't resist my charm." He threw his best smile at her.

"What if—"

"Sarah, relax. It's all going to work out. Then you can have your life back." He winced at the thought. What if they didn't want to give her up? What if he and the twins just kept her? But that thought was ridiculous. She wasn't some homeless puppy who had wandered into their yard. Sarah had a life of her own.

"My brother and Melody are getting married, did I tell you?" she chattered.

"Three or four times."

He could feel the hot glare she shot his way and chuckled unrepentantly.

"Melody is pregnant."

He slammed on the brakes. The car behind them blared their horn. "Don't do that to me."

She smirked. "Just wanted to make sure you were listening. So, are you ready to be an uncle again?"

"I doubt we'll still be married by the time she has a baby."

"Oh, you never know," Sarah said mysteriously.

He frowned. She shouldn't joke about the fleeting nature of their marriage. If the twins believed she was going to stay forever, it would break their hearts when she finally left. If he allowed himself to believe she might stay forever, it just might break his heart, too.

Chapter Fourteen

The twins tumbled from the front door of Trent's house and launched themselves at Sarah.

" 'Arah Mommy?" Kyle asked breathlessly.

"They've been so excited that you married Trent. I believe they know every word we said." Melody laughed, her hand resting lightly on her stomach.

Melody's face glowed, her cheeks almost rosy. Ryan deserved to be happy, and Sarah was pretty certain Melody loved him. Her expression was downright sappy when she gazed up at him. She hoped she didn't look at Trent that way, or he would send her packing even sooner than planned.

"Mama." Caitlin's tone rang out decisively as she, too, toddled over to Sarah.

Tears formed in Sarah's eyes. These two precious children called her *Mother,* a word she'd thought she'd never hear. She wanted to hold them close and never lose this moment. It was a rare picture in time, one that she wouldn't soon forget.

"Sarah isn't staying forever, guys." He stopped at her side and knelt down to the twins' level. "She's only here temporarily."

His words cut swift and deep. Sarah's chest tightened as she struggled for the next breath. He took a hand in each of his big strong ones and walked into the house with the twins. She stared after him, stricken. Of course she knew he didn't plan for their marriage to be permanent, but hearing it again hurt. The moment with the twins was one she'd dreamed of for years, and Trent had just blown the dream into a million tiny bits.

She met Ryan's eyes. He shrugged. "Sorry, Sis. Maybe he'll come around."

Melody bit her lip and avoided Sarah's gaze. A woman could always tell the truth, and Melody saw what Sarah had just discovered—Trent wasn't capable of loving her. She was just a means to keeping the twins and nothing more.

Setting her shoulders, she walked over the threshold into her temporary home. While it lasted, she would make the most of this family. They would remain hers in her heart even if they weren't in her life.

Fury pumped through Trent's veins. He would not allow the twins to be hurt by anyone. What had Sarah's brother been thinking by telling them they were getting a new mother?

"Melissa can't be replaced," he muttered to himself. Not only that, but the marriage wasn't real. How was he going to explain to these two children, who'd already suffered devastating losses, that Sarah was leaving, too?

"Twent." Caitlin hugged his legs.

She had followed them into the house and stood uncertainly by the front door. What was he going to do with her? He didn't have a spare bedroom, and he could hardly tell her to go home, when the social worker could show up any minute.

"Should I go home until the court investigator shows up?" Her chin was held at that haughty angle, and her lashes swept her cheeks in a slow arc.

He'd hurt her feelings, Trent realized. The lashes were a dead giveaway. It seemed as though he was always saying or doing the wrong thing lately. His life was impossible. He couldn't please everyone, and he certainly couldn't please Sarah.

"No. You should stay here."

She still stood by the doorway, as though unconvinced.

"If the social worker shows up, she'll think it funny if you aren't here."

She shrugged. "Okay."

They had been close until he'd pulled the twins from her and stalked into the house. He frowned. He instinctively rebuilt the wall between them, but as Sarah said in Vegas, there was no reason why they couldn't be friends.

"Are you hungry?" she asked.

Taking over her wifely duties already, Trent thought. But that wasn't fair. She was putting her life on hold to help him keep the twins. So, why did he feel as though there was a noose around his neck, and it was tightening with each ticking second?

"Dinner would be nice."

She stared blankly at him. "Well, don't look at me. I'm used to cooking soup and peanut butter and jelly."

That surprised a chuckle out of him, which lessened the tension in the air. "I suppose you expect me to feed you?"

"We have to eat, don't we?" she reasoned as she walked farther into the room.

She still looked uncomfortable, though, and Trent realized that if she was forced to live with them for the next few weeks, he was going to have to help her feel at home.

"Look, Sarah, I overreacted outside. It was just that I didn't want the twins to be hurt when they lost another person they love. Do you understand?"

"Sure."

She was acting nonchalant, but he could tell she'd been hurt. Despite her protests, she was a traditionalist at heart.

That worthless fiancé's desertion wouldn't still haunt her if she didn't believe in love and family and happily-ever-after. Traditions were important to Sarah.

Traditions. He stared at the closed front door in trepidation. He hadn't carried her over the threshold. Something he was certain Sarah had noticed even if she hadn't commented on it.

This might not be a real marriage, but Sarah said she wanted to experience it while she had the chance. That's what the strawberries and champagne were about. He remembered her soft, full mouth settling onto the fruit, and his body stirred in response. He wondered if she wanted to experience all the benefits of marriage? Thoughts like that were best left alone.

Making a decision he would probably regret the minute he touched her, Trent scooped her into his arms and headed out the front door.

"Trent, what are you doing?" She squealed and grabbed his shoulders to balance herself. "Are you throwing me out already?"

"Don't be ridiculous. I'm going to carry you over the threshold." Only grim determination kept him from making his arousal painfully apparent.

"Oh." Sarah's smile grew dreamy, and she relaxed in his arms.

What was going on in that pretty head of hers? Was she imagining that he was someone else, and she was living a happily-ever-after fantasy? She certainly looked like she'd traveled to fantasyland.

She could no more have avoided falling in love with Trent than she could control her hunger for double chocolate chunk ice cream, she realized. That he'd thought to carry her over the threshold, even after the fact, only reminded her of how sensitive he was underneath. She tightened her arms around his neck and wished she never had to let go.

"Don't you think you should open your eyes, Sarah?"

She sighed and snuggled closer. "Why? I don't need to see where I'm going."

"Should I open my eyes?" He pretended to bump into the door.

She laughed and heard the twins clap their hands and giggle.

"I love you, Trent Kasey." Might as well get that out of the way. Now was as a good a time as any.

He lowered her, letting her body slide down his in a sensuous dance. His eyes turned to a deep smoky green. Had he heard her confession?

"I'll go start dinner." He pulled back and walked away.

She sighed. He'd heard her all right. The question was, what did he plan to do about it?

He couldn't have heard her right. But he had. She had said she loved him. She hadn't meant it though. Not in that way. It had been a joking, you're-a-great-guy-and-a-friend "I love you." Not a passionate, I'd-die-without-you "I love you."

That's all she'd meant. Or was it? Was it possible that Sarah meant she really loved him? Or did she just want him? Why had she agreed to marry him anyway? That was a question he intended to ask her. As soon as possible.

Chapter Fifteen

The smell of scorched pancakes filled the air, Kyle's forehead swelled with a lump already the size of an egg, even the dog refused to eat the pancakes, and Caitlin colored on the wall with a red crayon.

She was a total failure as a wife and mother. Scooping Kyle into her arms, she rescued the crayon from Caitlin. Caring for the twins twenty-four hours a day was a big adjustment.

"C'mon, guys. The social worker will be here any minute. Your uncle isn't home yet. I need your help."

Kyle wailed louder. She patted him on the back, wondering where the pounding sound was coming from. Her head ached as the sound grew louder, reverberating like echoes in her head.

The front door! Why isn't the doorbell working? Unless it's Trent. Did he forget his key? Why doesn't he just ring the bell! She swung the door open and wished she could sink through the clay tiles.

"Is Mr. Kasey home?" The woman's thick brown hair was scraped back from her face in a tight knot at the back of her head.

"I'm afraid not." She bit her lip. *Of all the lousy timing . . .*

"Humph. We had an appointment." The woman clicked her pen open and jotted something in her notebook. "May I ask who you are?"

"I'm terribly sorry. Won't you please come in?" She stood aside while the woman stomped past in slingback pumps. "I—that is we—knew you were coming of course.

He was supposed to be back. I can't imagine what's keeping him."

The woman sniffed the air, wrinkling her nose. "What is that smell?"

She gasped. "My pancakes!" Setting Kyle on the couch, she ran for the kitchen.

Black smoke billowed from the frying pan, and her pancakes resembled two flat pieces of charcoal. Tears weren't an option or Sarah would have quit at that moment and collapsed onto the blue-and-white linoleum.

Instead, she moved the smoldering pan from the burner to the sink and ran cold water in it. Turning on the exhaust fan, she returned to the living room, where Caitlin had resumed her masterpiece in crayon on the wall and Kyle had joined her with his own purple crayon.

"Kyle. Caitlin. Give me the crayons." She held her hand out.

The twins offered two sheepish grins and gave up the crayons. She quickly popped in a *Barney* tape, and they settled down like the perfect angels they weren't.

She turned back to the social worker, who scribbled more notes in her little journal. No doubt writing the details of what a horrible mother figure Sarah was.

"Ms. Walters, I'm so sorry about this mess. I'm afraid I'm still getting used to cooking for more than one."

"Hmmm." The woman kept scribbling.

"Trent should be back any minute."

"Hmmm."

Well, Ms. Walters was quite the conversationalist. She allowed the silence to drag on for several moments while the background filled with a child's song about bubble gum on a bedpost.

"I don't believe we've established who you are." It was

121

the first thing the woman had said in over ten minutes.

She jumped at the sharp words. Did the woman suspect her reasons for being there? What if she saw right through the charade and realized they only married to retain custody of the twins? Would the court automatically take Caitlin and Kyle away for treachery or something?

"I'm Mrs. Kasey." She waited for a reaction, but was sorely disappointed. Apparently, Ms. Walters was a trained professional and didn't show emotions.

"There is no mention of a wife in my notes." Her gray eyes were as chilly as an Arctic winter.

"We only married recently."

"I see."

A few more scribbled notes.

"Mrs. Kasey, why shouldn't I find it suspect that you would marry Mr. Kasey just before his court hearing? You and I both know it will improve his chances of retaining custody."

She took a deep breath. She'd prepared an answer for this. She'd known the marriage would look suspicious.

"Ms. Walters, I love Trent Kasey. I love Caitlin and Kyle, too." Her throat closed off, making her next words come out choked. "I love them as if they were my own children."

And it was the truth. Why else would she put up with burnt pancake aroma and red-and-purple walls? She loved this family and would do whatever was necessary to protect them. That included testifying on the stand as to what a cold, bitter woman Ms. Walters was.

"Hmmm." Ms. Walters scribbled a few more notes. "May I see their bedroom?"

"Certainly." She stood, but hesitated to leave Caitlin and Kyle alone. They could get into trouble within seconds, and the timing couldn't be worse. "Caitlin, Kyle, come show the nice lady your room."

Kyle's thumb found his mouth, and Caitlin immediately grabbed her blankie, but they both followed. The bedroom was simple, but filled with toys and games to stimulate their young minds and chubby fingers. Two toddler beds rested catty-corner from one another in the far corner, and stuffed animals filled a low-lying window bench. A bucket of Legos lay turned on its side in the middle of the room. She quickly rescued it, returned the stray pieces to the bucket, and placed it on a shelf.

"Adequate." The woman scribbled some more.

Adequate? What in the world would she call squalor? The room was everything many children dreamed of. He obviously put a lot of thought and planning into what would be comfortable and a room they could grow into.

She tightened her lips and bit down on her steadily growing anger. It was important she make a good impression on this woman, and flaring up at her wouldn't help matters.

"May I offer you some refreshments, Ms. Walters?" She smiled sweetly.

"No, thank you."

Strike number nine hundred. Where was Trent? She couldn't do this by herself. She was going to lose the twins. He would never forgive her. She'd never forgive herself.

Glancing at her watch, the woman clicked the pen. "It's a shame Mr. Kasey couldn't keep his appointment. I'm afraid I'll have to base my findings on my interview with you."

That was it. She couldn't hold her tongue any longer. "Please, Ms. Walters. I'm sure the only thing that would have detained Trent was an absolute emergency. These children mean everything to him. Everything."

"But supposedly he has you, Mrs. Kasey." The woman stared at her with suspicious eyes. "Surely you want children of your own."

It was none of the woman's business. Something that Sarah rarely shared with anyone, but if her barrenness could help . . .

"I can't have children of my own, Ms. Walters. And, even if I could, it wouldn't make a difference. You see, I love these two."

The sound of the front door slamming made Sarah's heart shift back into neutral. Thank God. It had to be Trent.

"Trent, is that you?" Did her voice sound as nervous to Ms. Walters as it did to her?

"Sarah, sorry I'm late. There was a terrible accident, and I stopped to help."

His broad shoulders filled the doorway, his anxious green eyes taking in the scene. He smiled warmly at Ms. Walters and held out his hand.

"I must apologize if I've inconvenienced you, Ms. Walters. I see you've met my wife Sarah."

If she had not seen it with her own eyes, she would have called anyone telling the story a liar. Ms. Walters melted like an ice cube on a hot July afternoon. She let her hand linger in Trent's a moment too long and batted her lashes. The hussy actually batted her lashes!

"Actually, I think I have everything I need, Mr. Kasey, so it isn't a problem at all."

It wasn't? Was this the same woman who had insinuated only moments before that he hadn't cared enough to keep the appointment? Good grief.

She trailed the woman and Trent to the front door. She

would have given ten years off her life to see what was in that notebook the woman kept scribbling in. Perhaps she'd add a few lines of poetry about Trent's charm?

Shocked at her jealousy, Sarah forced a smile for the woman. Since when had she grown so possessive? Or was it simply that she didn't have any real hold on him, so she resented any snippet of civility he gave to someone else?

He closed the door and turned to Sarah. "I think that went pretty well."

To her absolute horror she burst into tears. He pulled her into his arms and rubbed soothing circles over her back.

"What's wrong?"

"I made a total mess of it, that's what's wrong. If you lose the twins, it'll be all my f-fault." She hiccuped on the last word.

"It couldn't have been that bad."

"You don't have a clue."

He walked her over to the couch, keeping an arm around her shoulders. "So tell me about it."

He lowered them to the couch and pulled her to his side.

"When she walked in, Kyle had a huge lump on his forehead, Caitlin was coloring on the wall, and pancakes were burning in the kitchen."

He chuckled.

"It's not funny, Trent. I'm telling you, she was far from impressed with me. And you weren't here, I didn't know what to say."

"It's going to work out, Sarah. Trust me. She was as impressed as she was likely to get. She had to see how hard you're trying."

"Trying only counts in board games." She felt the corners of her lips turn down. Why couldn't she do anything right for this family?

"I know what will cheer you up," he said.

"What? Are they giving out wife lessons?"

"You don't need them. We're going out to dinner."

"With the twins?"

"Of course. We're a family."

She felt a tiny flutter in her heart. He'd called them a family. Even if it was temporary, he had still said it.

"I think you're insane, but let's go for it."

"I'll go get the twins ready while you change clothes." He paused and looked at her slightly faded jeans and knit cable shirt. "On second thought, you look perfect."

She laughed. "I take it this isn't a fancy dinner."

"With two kids under two years of age? Are you insane?"

"I married you, didn't I?"

"Touché, darling." He left the room whistling.

Too bad she'd never learned to whistle. A duet might have been fun.

The local pizza parlor was just noisy enough to cover the excited chatter of Caitlin and Kyle. Sarah allowed herself to relax for the first time since that morning.

"The court hearing is set for next Friday. Do you think one of your brothers can watch the twins?"

"Ryan already offered. I think he's trying to get in plenty of practice before his baby arrives."

Caitlin discovered her fork and started to bang noisily on the Formica table. Sarah reached over and rescued the fork, replacing it with a multicolored plastic sign that would do less damage.

"Do you really think the hearing will go okay?" She pleated her napkin into a dozen almost even folds and began to unpleat it again.

"Honest?"

"It's always the best policy."

"I don't know." He ran his hand over Kyle's silky black hair, and Sarah noticed that his fingers trembled the tiniest bit.

She reached over and laid her hand on top of his other clenched fist. "It's going to work out. They can't help but see how loved those two are."

"Thanks, Sarah. I know you've really put your life on hold for us."

She waved her hand. "It's nothing." But it was everything. These three human beings held her heart and her happiness in their hands.

"Don't do that." He raised her hand to his lips and kissed the back of her knuckles.

Sarah's breath hitched in her throat, and all the heat in her settled in the lower regions of her body.

"Without you, I wouldn't have had a chance."

"Glad to be of help." Glad wasn't quite the word. Without this marriage, she would never have known the joy of being a mother. Yes, it was difficult. The twins were energetic and wore her out before noon each day. But it was also the only thing she'd ever done that had truly fulfilled her. Raising two precious human beings was more of a gift than Trent could imagine.

"I'm still trying to figure out how to juggle my clients and the twins though. I'm thinking of turning my house into a training center. I'll have to see if my landlord would be willing to sell."

"As soon as the hearing is over, you'll have more freedom." His words fell like heavy droplets of acid, bursting her rose-colored bubbles.

Chapter Sixteen

"It's a beautiful night for sitting on the front porch," she told him.

"Uh-huh." He kept his gaze on the television.

She knew he wasn't interested in the cartoon about dragons. She crossed her arms and glared at him.

"I'm going to take Night for a walk, I guess. I'll be back."

"Okay."

As if he really cared. She slammed the front door behind her. Night was waiting for her in the side yard Trent had fenced in a few days ago. The dog was used to having her in the same house, and since he was a social breed, the separation from her was hard on him. They tried to allow him in the house as much as possible, but he was getting large, and it became crowded when they were all home. Luckily they spent a lot of time outside. His tail thumped noisily against the wall.

"Hi, baby. Wanna go for a walk?"

Night made a tight circle and barked.

"You're always happy to see me, aren't you, boy?"

She stroked the strong black head. If only a man could love the way her dog did, with absolute, unquestioning devotion. Not just any man, her husband.

After a long walk on the beach, Sarah reluctantly left Night in his new doghouse and went back inside. Night would probably dig up every petunia she and the twins had planted, but it would only be because he was lonely.

She knew exactly how he felt. She'd never imagined she could feel so lonely living in a house full of people.

★ ★ ★ ★ ★

Trent breathed a sigh of relief when Sarah walked out the door. He could let his guard down for a few moments. Having her in the same house was wearing on him. He'd given her his bedroom and taken the couch, but it hadn't helped restrain his thoughts.

The front door opened, then slammed with force. He winced.

"I'm back." She collapsed in an armchair.

"So I heard."

"You want to fight, Trent?" She narrowed her eyes. "Because I'm in the mood."

The passion blazed in her eyes. God she was beautiful. "Has anyone ever told you that your eyes turn navy blue when you're angry?"

"Don't do that."

"Do what?" He couldn't figure this woman out, so why did he even try?

"Distract me with a compliment when I'm trying to be angry with you."

"You have to try to get mad at me?" He laughed.

"You haven't said two words to me all night." She crossed her arms.

He knew exactly where this was leading, and he refused to go there. "Did I tell you I have another meeting with Rick Matthews? He may have another job for me."

Trent's gaze dropped to Sarah's lips, remembering what it tasted like to cover them with his own.

"Tell me about the new job with Matthews," she said.

He covered his laugh with a cough. She wanted to be angry with him, but couldn't seem to maintain it.

"He has narrowed this latest job down to three contractors. We meet again Wednesday to discuss details."

"That's good."

"It's great. Rick Matthews is one of the largest developers in this area. Steady contracts with him mean regular work, raises for all my workers, and plenty of college money for Caitlin and Kyle."

"You're right. It's wonderful." She leaned forward and placed her hand on his arm.

Heat followed the touch of her skin, setting him on fire. He wanted to scoop her into his arms and take her into his bedroom. His gaze dropped to her full lips again, and, before he could stop himself, he leaned over and kissed her.

Sarah leaned into him, responding with enough heat to set the house ablaze. Trent pulled back a little. "We shouldn't."

Sarah swallowed several times, her eyes glazed over with passion.

"Let's celebrate." She jumped to her feet. "I'll go pick up a pizza."

"Fancy." He grinned, feeling more content than he had a right to feel. More content than he should feel.

"We could have champagne with it," she suggested.

"And strawberries?" What devil had made him say that?

Sarah's gaze fell to his lips. She wet hers with the moist, pink tip of her tongue.

"If you want."

Oh, he wanted. Wanted but couldn't touch, and that was the entire problem. The marriage was temporary. He couldn't handle losing anyone else, and it would be all too easy to fall in love with Sarah.

She was tired of pretending. Tired of trying to keep her distance from Trent physically and emotionally. What would his reaction be if she threw herself into his arms the minute he walked into the door and kissed him until he begged for mercy?

"He'd probably pack my bags and set me on the doorstep." She peeled potatoes. "At least I can feed him a great dinner. The way to a man's heart and all that."

The twins would be up from their nap soon, she needed to get the rest of the meal on the stove.

"Sarah. I'm home." Trent's voice followed the sound of the front door slamming.

She rushed to the kitchen door and put her hands on her hips. "You're early," she accused.

"Nice to see you, too."

"I didn't mean that. It's just that—" Just why did she turn into a blithering idiot when he was around? "I was cooking a special dinner to celebrate your meeting with Rick Matthews. It isn't ready yet."

"How do you know if I got the contract or not? I won't even know for a few days."

"Doesn't matter. You were a finalist. That's worth celebrating."

He laughed, and Sarah's heart gave that funny kick it often gave when he was around. Deep grooves of mirth transformed his face. She loved him. She took several deep, painful breaths.

"I'd better go finish dinner. Do you want to get the twins? They're in their room."

"Sure."

He moved to the twins' room, and Sarah turned back toward the kitchen and her potatoes. Life moved on just as it did each time there was an opportunity for them to share a special connection.

"One of us always turns away," she whispered.

"Sarah is talking to herself again, guys." He had entered

the room with a twin in each arm. Sarah had been so lost in thought, she hadn't heard them.

She felt the heat creep up her face. Had he heard what she'd said?

He picked up a potato. "I'll help peel."

"My hero." She handed him the potato peeler and opened the oven to check on the pot roast. "I'll try not to burn anything."

"I'm thinking of buying a new couch. One with a foldout bed."

What would he say if she told him she thought they ought to share his bed? "Why don't you let me buy it? It's the least I can do after Princess destroyed your other one."

"What do you think about a Hide-A-Bed, Sarah?" Trent's gaze fell to her mouth.

She took a deep breath and dived in headfirst. "I think you should just share with me."

Trent's eyes glazed over. She wished she knew if it was from shock or desire.

Lying in bed next to Trent but not being able to touch him was pure torture. Why had she ever suggested such an arrangement? She could feel the heat of his body across the few inches that separated them.

She flipped over, turning her back to him. It didn't help. She sighed.

"What's wrong, Sarah?" His voice wrapped around her across the darkness. The deep rhythm of his voice was as arousing as a stroke.

"I can't sleep."

"Maybe this will help." The feel of his strong hands stroking her back was about as soothing as molten lava erupting from a volcano.

"Better?" he asked.

Only if he stroked the rest of her body, too. She only had to survive until the hearing without making a total fool of herself. Within minutes she heard his steady breathing and realized he'd dropped off to sleep.

Chapter Seventeen

If prayers were dollars, Trent Kasey'd own the entire town. Then there would be no need to fight Nathan Winters in court, he could simply sign over whatever amount it took to get Nathan Winters out of their lives.

"Nervous?" Sarah's eyes were robin's-egg blue that day, set off by the tailored navy dress suit she wore.

"Does it show?" He adjusted his tie.

She pushed his hand out of the way and tightened the knot. "Only to me."

Sarah's mother leaned over the bench behind him, and whispered, "We're all rooting for you, Trent."

He swallowed several times before he could speak.

"Thank you all for coming today." Sarah's family filled the row directly behind their table. Maybe the show of support would help sway the judge?

"I wish this were over." What if he lost custody? He'd never get another night's sleep. Every second would be spent worrying over Caitlin and Kyle.

"There he is," Sarah whispered.

Nathan Winters strolled down the courtroom aisle, glared at Trent, and leaned over to whisper to his lawyer before sitting down. A girl who looked barely nineteen pulled out her own chair and sat beside him. Her eyes were wide and she kept twisting her hands together. She must be Winters' wife. Trent worried that she would even know how to take care of herself, much less Caitlin and Kyle. He could only assume she was here for show as it was the first time he'd seen her.

"Where is my lawyer?" Gregg Roberts was late, with a capital L.

"I don't know, but I think the judge is ready to start." She nodded to the front of the courtroom, where a bailiff had opened the chamber door.

"This isn't going well at all." He was trapped in a nightmare he couldn't wake up from. His odds were fifty-fifty of winning the twins if Gregg Roberts was there. What were the odds without a lawyer?

They rose for the judge's entrance; still no Gregg. The judge plopped down on his high-backed chair and settled his voluminous robes. Peering over his glasses, his gaze focused first on Sarah, then Trent.

"Mr. Kasey, you're choosing to represent yourself today?"

He stood and cleared his throat. "Your Honor, my lawyer is running late. Is there any way we could have a continuance?"

Please, God, let there be a continuance. More time with the twins. More time with Sarah.

"I'm afraid not, Mr. Kasey. We've already postponed this hearing once. If your lawyer isn't inclined to be prompt, the court can't be responsible—"

The courtroom door creaked open, and Gregg Roberts rushed down the aisle. "Sorry I'm late. Terrible traffic."

Trent glared at him. The judge raised his brows but didn't comment.

"Who is this young lady with you?" The judge frowned at Sarah as if she were an added aggravation he didn't need.

He placed a protective arm around Sarah's shoulders. "This is my wife."

"You have a wife?"

Gregg Roberts stood. "I have a copy of the marriage license, Your Honor."

"Let's see it." The judge wiggled impatient fingers, and Gregg Roberts passed the paper over to the eager judge.

"Quite recent. Tell me, young lady, why did you marry Trent Kasey? Perhaps to help his court case? Hmmm?"

Wonderful. Just his luck to get a judge who refused to let anyone pull the wool over his eyes. Just once, Trent would've liked to be given the benefit of the doubt. Especially since the judge was right on the mark. What would Sarah say?

"I love Trent, Your Honor." Sarah's voice rang out clear and strong. Her words didn't waver.

He swallowed. She hadn't told an outright lie. She loved him like a friend. She'd already made that clear. Would the judge take her words at their basic value, or would he want her to clarify?

"That's not exactly what I asked, is it?" The judge removed his spectacles and rubbed his fingers against his left temple.

"Migraine, Your Honor?" she asked.

The judge started in surprise; then his lips hitched up in the vaguest of smiles. "Just starting."

"If I might offer a tip, sir. If you'll take Tylenol with some caffeine, it may knock it out."

The judge actually smiled, and Trent felt the coil of tension loosen the tiniest bit. At least the man seemed to like Sarah. Surely that would work in his favor.

"This is ridiculous. Could we get on with the hearing?" Nathan Winters grumbled. "I'd like to take my children home."

"And who is the young woman with you, Mr. Winters?" The judge leaned back and crossed his arms.

"My wife."

The judge shuffled some paperwork. "Seems you

were married recently, too."

The judge stared at Winters's wife. "Young lady, do you have anything to add?"

She shook her head and mumbled, "No, sir."

"Very well. Mr. Roberts, I have your brief, would you like to add anything else?" He turned to Trent's lawyer.

"Your Honor, Trent Kasey was clearly Melissa's choice as a guardian for her children. Not only did she leave a will naming him legal guardian, but the biological father, Mr. Nathan Winters, has never been involved in their lives." Gregg Roberts spoke up.

"I object." Nathan Winters's attorney jumped to his feet.

"What exactly is it you are objecting to?" the judge asked.

"Mr. Winters has not given up his parental rights."

"In this court, I like to work on facts and gut instinct. I'm a bit famous for it." The judge chuckled, then cleared his throat. "Mr. Winters, why should I let you have custody of these children?"

Nathan Winters's gaze darted around nervously before settling on his lawyer. The lawyer nodded encouragement for Nathan to answer the judge.

"Melissa kept me from the kids. I want to be a father."

"That's a lie," Trent said under his breath.

Sarah wrapped her arm through his and squeezed his biceps, trying to calm him. Trent wondered if she could feel the tense muscles in his arm.

"My wife and I want to raise the children. Isn't that right, honey?" Winters grabbed the girl's arm and hauled her to her feet. She nodded quickly.

"Do you plan to have children of your own? Is your wife prepared to take on two children she doesn't know and isn't related to? How will Caitlin and Kyle fit your plans?" the judge said.

"We hadn't really thought about it." Nathan stuck his hands in his pockets and rocked back on his heels.

"Would you be willing to consent to some supervised visits so the children can get to know you and you them?"

"Yeah, I guess." Nathan Winters didn't seem too certain. "I'd be in control of their money, too, right?"

The judge pulled his spectacles down and stared at Nathan Winters for a moment before turning his attention back to his notes. "Mr. Winters, it says here that you will grant Mr. Kasey custody if you can be executor of Melissa Kasey's estate, which consists of a house and an insurance policy. Your lawyer has very cleverly worded the brief to state that you do not feel the same person should be in charge of the money and the children. My question to you is which do you want to be in charge of, the money or the children?"

Nathan Winters darted a panicked look to his lawyer. The lawyer mouthed something, and Winters turned back to the judge. "Both."

The judge sighed and shook his head. "That would hardly separate the two, would it?" He turned to Trent.

"Mr. Kasey, why do you want the children?" The judge's gaze fell to their entwined arms.

Sarah moved away slowly. Trent knew she didn't want the judge to think she was putting on a show for the courtroom.

"I love Caitlin and Kyle, Your Honor. I loved Melissa. She wanted me to raise them."

"Is there anything else, Mr. Kasey?"

Trent pursed his lips, glanced at Nathan Winters, then shook his head.

"Your Honor." Gregg Roberts stood. "Two months ago, Mr. Winters contacted my client and offered to sever his parental rights for a fee."

"Indeed?" The judge's bushy gray eyebrows rose. "Mr. Winters?"

Nathan Winters's attorney stood. "My client declines comment on this outlandish charge."

"I do not," Nathan Winters yelled.

"Let it go." His lawyer placed a hand on his shoulder and Winters seemed to calm a bit.

"Liar." Nathan sat back down but continued to glare at Trent and Sarah.

The judge turned toward Trent and Sarah. "According to the report I read, it seems you're not a very good cook, Mrs. Kasey."

She winced. "I'm afraid not, Your Honor. I'm used to cooking for one. I'm learning, though."

"Mr. Winters, would you like to add anything else before we recess? Anything at all?"

Nathan Winters stood. "Sir, Your Honor, I want to raise my kids. That's all I want. A man should have that right. They are *mine* after all. Just because their mother kept me from them is no reason I should be kept from them forever."

The judge nodded. "I'll need a few hours to deliberate. Both sides present a strong case, and any decision that involves children should not be taken lightly. Let's break for lunch and return at two this afternoon, when I will render my final decision."

"If he reads that report, we're sunk." She frowned.

"Maybe we're sunk anyway."

Gregg Roberts turned to them. "Why don't you two go have lunch and try not to worry?" He walked away.

"I'm not sure I like your lawyer, Trent."

"I know what you mean, but he was the best I could afford."

"Let's hope he makes it back on time."

"We should probably eat." Catherine laid her hand on Sarah's arm.

"I'm not hungry. Are you?" She chewed on her bottom lip.

"No, but we have several hours to kill."

He wasn't sure how he was going to stay calm. A million what-ifs were running through his mind. What if the twins were taken away? What if Nathan Winters abused them? What if he stole their money, then deserted them, would Trent be allowed to take them in? What if, by some small miracle, he was allowed to keep them? Either way, Sarah would leave. That was another issue he didn't want to face at the moment. He'd gotten far too used to having her around.

The hamburger tasted like sawdust. She forced herself to chew and swallow. Chew and swallow.

Trent looked as though he were enjoying his lunch about as much as she was.

"What are our options if the judge decides in Nathan Winters's favor?" Sarah asked.

"An appeal. Gregg said the twins would more than likely stay with us until the appeals were exhausted."

"How many appeals? How much time?" She laid the hamburger down. She couldn't eat. She couldn't lose the twins. She couldn't lose Trent.

"I think two more appeals. Timing depends on how burdened the court is. How long it takes for a hearing." Trent's mouth turned down at the corners. "It wouldn't surprise me if I lost them."

"Don't say that." She felt the negative energy swirling around them.

"I've lost everyone I've ever loved."

In that moment, he looked like a lonely twelve-year-old who'd just lost his parents. She reached across the table and laid her hands on top of his.

"Then it's about time for your luck to change." Sarah's father turned from the big-screen TV he'd focused on since their entrance.

"What if it's a curse?" he whispered. "What if I'm meant to be alone?"

She sucked in her breath. His words hit so close to her own thoughts that his pain became her own.

"Everything will work out." It had to.

She didn't want to hear the decision. If he lost the twins, it could very well be her fault. She had made a terrible impression on the social worker, there was no doubt about it. The judge also knew why she'd married Trent. The man wasn't a fool, and Sarah was certain he'd seen right through their hasty marriage.

If Trent was given custody, and Sarah prayed with every breath that he would be, that would mean her marriage was over. She wasn't ready to leave. Her time with Trent and the twins had been so short. Just a few weeks more. She wanted time to build some memories to see her through the rest of her life. How would she ever survive being without them?

Gregg Roberts twirled a pencil between his fingers like a minibaton, banging the eraser end against the heavy wood table every few seconds.

She wanted to rip it out of his hands and snap it in two. However, that probably wouldn't create the best impression on the judge either.

"Sarah, about our marriage," he whispered.

She swallowed. She didn't want to hear this. What would everyone think if she suddenly threw her hands over her ears? What a childish thought, but she couldn't help it. She wasn't ready to be cut out of his life like a bad spot in an apple.

"Not now, Trent." She kept her gaze on the judge as he continued to shuffle paperwork, not looking at any of them.

"But, I wanted to talk to you before—"

"It wasn't an easy decision." The judge's voice interrupted Trent, and Sarah breathed a sigh of relief.

If she could continue to avoid the issue, he couldn't throw her out of his life. How long could she keep that up though?

She crossed her fingers under the table. Despite the fact that she was losing Trent and the twins, she wanted him to keep custody. *Please, God, please. Don't let those sweet little angels go to that horrid man, who doesn't love them. Anything but that. They deserve to be loved.*

"Let me say that while this court recognizes the rights of the biological father, it also recognizes the wishes of the mother. A mother who cared for her children with no help from the father. Because the children do not know their father and the mother specifically requested they be raised by her brother, I have decided the children will remain in the custody of their uncle, Trent Kasey, and his wife, with the condition of regular visits from the social worker to check on the children's progress."

"Thank God." Trent's words were husky.

"However, since this court recognizes that biological parents have rights, Mr. Winters, should you wish it, the court will order visitation privileges."

No! If the court allowed the kids to visit Nathan Winters

and he harmed them . . .

"Mr. Winters declines visitation," the lawyer stated.

She grabbed Trent's arm in excitement. *It can't be this easy. We've won!* The twins were safe. She and Trent had done it, together, as a team.

The second the judge passed through the chamber door, Sarah threw herself into Trent's arms, laughing happily.

"We did it. The twins are yours."

He smiled. "Sarah, I don't know how to thank you." He lowered his lips to hers.

They'd shared a few kisses, each a little more passionate than the first, building upon one another. This kiss was different, holding an element the other kisses hadn't. Softer, gentler, but with no less passion. It was as if in that moment their souls reached out to one another and embraced.

When the kiss ended, they stared at one another, speechless. She wanted to beg him to let her stay, but she wouldn't unless he asked her to. The reason for their marriage was over, and it was only a matter of time until Trent realized that.

"Don't think this is over." The hateful hiss of Nathan Winters broke the spell they were under.

"It's over, Winters." His body tensed as he turned to face Nathan Winters.

His sudden alertness reminded Sarah of a feral wild dog. Every muscle in Trent's body had tensed, and even his teeth were slightly bared. He was the head of the pack, protecting his pups.

"Wrong. I don't lose, boy. The lawyer already has an appeal ready to file."

"He can't do that," Sarah gasped.

Nathan Winters stalked out of the courtroom, the wooden door sputtering shut behind him.

"Obviously he can, Sarah." He was staring thoughtfully after Winters. "It's unlikely he'll overturn the decision unless he can prove one of us unfit."

"That shouldn't be too hard, if they look at me." She wondered what all was in that social worker's report.

"You're a misfit, not unfit."

"Thanks a lot."

He sat in the chair next to her and took her hands in his. "Sarah, the real issue here is what this means to you."

"I don't understand."

"Our marriage will have to continue indefinitely. How do you feel about that?"

Ecstatic, that was how she felt. But she could hardly say that. Indefinitely. That was the next best thing to forever in this particular marriage.

He hadn't known Sarah could sing. She sang a lullaby clear and strong to the twins. He'd heard Kyle's screams, as he'd heard them at least once a week since Melissa died.

"Hush, little baby . . ."

He stood in the darkened hallway and watched the soft light from the bedside lamp cast a golden glow over Sarah's long curls. God, she was beautiful. She raised her hand and brushed her fingers down Kyle's cheek.

"All better now?" she asked.

Trent's throat ached at the tenderness in her expression. She was meant to be a mother. Nature had played a cruel trick when she'd stolen that chance from this woman.

"Blankie," Caitlin demanded.

"Did you lose your blankie?" She grabbed the tattered blanket from the floor and tucked it into Caitlin's hands.

She was meant to have children. *My children,* Trent thought possessively, as the image of a dark-haired infant crowded into his thoughts. But that wasn't possible.

"I love you, Caitlin." She leaned over and kissed his niece on the forehead. "I love you too, Kyle. You two are the best thing that's ever happened to me."

The longer Sarah stayed, the more attached she and the twins would be to each other. He knew he should feel guilty about extending this marriage. The truth was, he didn't. For so long, it seemed as though his life had been like that of a lone seagull, flying from place to place but with no real home.

First, Caitlin and Kyle had filled his home with brightness and love. Now Sarah was there, and it was as if overnight his life had been transformed. It was selfish, but a part of him wanted to hold on to the illusion of family as long as he could.

Everything he'd thought the world to be had turned out false. He'd been happy to float along life as a carefree bachelor. He hadn't been totally against marriage but had always thought of settling down as something in the far future.

She shut the door to the twins' bedroom softly behind her and bumped into Trent. His arms came up automatically to keep her from falling, and then he didn't want to release her.

"Trent, you scared me," she gasped.

His glance dropped to the deep vee of her silk pajama top. The dark shadow told him she wore nothing underneath, and the thought of what lay underneath the folds of red silk sent heat to his thighs.

"I was just listening to your lullaby. It usually takes me hours to calm them down. I don't sing as well as you do."

She laughed a soft, smoky laugh. "It's late."

"I'm not tired." His gaze fell to her mouth. Just one taste.

She licked her lips nervously, and he followed the movement. "Me either. Want some hot cocoa?"

"Not exactly what I had in mind, but I'll take what I can get."

She smiled shyly and turned for the kitchen. He followed her, wishing for things he had no right to wish for.

"I was thinking, Trent." Sarah's voice had the slightest catch in it, and he knew whatever she was about to say would change both of their lives forever.

Part of him wanted to keep such a change at bay, and his way of holding back unpleasant things had always been to joke his way out of them.

"That can be dangerous."

"I'm serious." She pinned him with her clear, blue gaze.

He sobered immediately. "Okay. I'm listening."

Stirring the cocoa, Sarah passed a mug to him and wrapped her fingers around her own cup, blowing on the surface to help cool the hot liquid.

He was certain she had no idea what scandalous thoughts her pursed lips were putting into his head.

"Would working more hours help build your company? Guarantee contracts with people like Rick Matthews?"

"It's suffered a little lately, I won't lie. But I'm not sure I want to work all the time. The twins are growing so fast as it is." Was she trying to find out how much money he had? He narrowed his eyes. He hadn't thought she'd be mercenary or ask for any type of settlement in a divorce, but how well did he really know Sarah? How well could you really ever know anyone?

"Eventually, you're going to have to devote more time to it, or risk losing money, am I right?" She was clutching the mug so tightly her knuckles were white.

"You're right."

146

He'd wait and see what she had to say. Whatever it was, it was obviously really important to her.

She took a deep breath and stood up straight. The mug of cocoa landed with a solid, decisive thump on the countertop.

"I want to continue as their nanny, even when—" She took a deep breath. "Even when our marriage is over."

"What?" The thought of their marriage being over hurt more than it should.

"You heard me. You'll need someone to care for them and I-I love them, Trent. Please, let me take care of them for you. Let me stay in their lives."

Tears trembled in the corners of her eyes like tiny crystals shimmering in the beams of a lighthouse.

"Let me get this straight . . . you want to give up your life to take care of my children?"

Sarah's smile was wobbly. "But you see, I won't be giving up anything. I'll be gaining two children I can never have. Trent, I already love them like they're my own. Try to find another caregiver who can say that. We already know how hard it is to find a decent nanny."

Trent could no more help pulling Sarah into his arms than he could help lowering his mouth to hers and drinking in her pureness of spirit. Sarah wrapped her arms around him and pressed closer, her breasts brushing against his chest.

Trent moaned low in his throat. He deepened the kiss, knowing he had to stop before it was too late to stop, yet not being able to. He moved from her mouth to her neck and Sarah gasped, her head falling back to allow him easier access.

With a strength of will he wasn't even aware he'd possessed, he set her gently away. There were too many things unspoken between them. Too many ways for an intimate encounter to go wrong, and they were headed down the path that led to heartache.

"Can I stay in their lives, Trent?" Sarah asked.

"We need to sleep, Sarah. We'll talk about this another time." But he had no intention of mentioning the subject again. She'd asked to be Kyle and Caitlin's nanny. All Trent wanted at that moment was for her to be his wife, in reality. Walking away was the hardest thing he'd ever done.

The day was perfect for a wedding. Bright sunshine spilled into the Goldwyne's backyard and glinted off the lacy bows Catherine Goldwyne tied to each metal chair back.

"The place looks terrific, Mom." She held Caitlin. Kyle clung to Trent's hand, his thumb in his mouth.

"I'm just so happy." Catherine burst into tears.

"Is everything okay?" He frowned.

"She really is just so happy, Trent." She rolled her eyes. Her mother had to want her children happily married more than any other mother in America. Maybe in the free world.

"Have you seen Melody?" Catherine threw her hand over her heart. "She looks beautiful."

"I think I'll go see if she needs help. I'm sure she's a nervous wreck." She handed Caitlin to Trent.

"If only I could have thrown you a big wedding."

She sighed. She'd almost made her escape before her mother started lamenting about missing planning her only daughter's wedding.

"Mother, the marriage is temporary. I keep telling you that. Now try to look happy. You're marrying off another child today."

"Two down. Two to go." Catherine turned back to the

bows. "Why don't you go and check on Melody, Sarah. I'm sure she's nervous. Since she doesn't have any family, the poor girl insisted on walking down the aisle by herself."

Sarah walked upstairs and to her old bedroom. Her mother had turned it into a sewing room, but an old-fashioned twin bed with yellow gauze netting and bright butterflies still sat in one corner. On the shelf next to the bed were favorite stuffed animals and books from Sarah's childhood.

It was almost as though her mother expected her to come home to live one day. Melody sat at a small white dressing table. Her face was as white as the gown she wore.

"Need help?" she asked.

"Got any Valium?"

She laughed. "No. But I took a class one time on relaxing with breathing exercises. Want to try some?"

"I can barely take in enough air to stay conscious I'm so nervous. Somehow I doubt I could handle exercises. Were you nervous, Sarah?"

"It doesn't count." She could feel the strain in her smile. "My marriage isn't real."

"What marriage is?" Melody's lips turned down at the corners.

"Hey. I'm supposed to be cheering you up." She walked to where Melody sat and bent over to give her a hug. "Welcome to the family. I hope you and Ryan will be very happy."

A single ray of sun peeked from behind the gathering clouds and hit him like a spotlight. He winced. Sarah's parents had claimed the twins, and he felt bare without them, as though everyone was staring, and he'd forgotten to put on an important piece of clothing.

"You hate this, don't you?" she whispered. The metal chairs had been pushed too close together, and her body brushed against his from her shoulder, to her side, to her thighs. He cleared his throat.

" 'Hate' is a strong word."

She laughed, the sound low and sultry and for his ears only. What was she doing to him?

"Relax. It shouldn't take long."

Trent's gaze focused on Sarah's moist lips. Just one little taste . . . The pianist pounded the beginning notes to the "Wedding March," shattering the moment.

"Ryan looks nervous," she whispered.

Sarah's brother stood stiffly, as though he were frozen in space and time. The only movement was a slight rocking from his heels to his tiptoes and back. Over and over. He barely remembered his own wedding day. At the time he'd believed it was because the marriage was temporary. Now he wasn't so sure. Had he been as nervous as Ryan?

The wedding guests rose as Melody stepped out of the French doors and started her walk to where her bridegroom was waiting. Her face was pasty white, but there was an element of joy on her face that made it almost glow.

He swallowed. The flowing white gown was topped with a frothy veil. An image of Sarah in her beaded gown pushed into his consciousness. Had he even told her she was beautiful that day?

"She's so beautiful." She squeezed his arm, and he thought he saw a tear on the end of her lashes.

Melody passed them and made her way to Ryan. Ryan turned to take the hand of his bride, and the look of pure devotion on his face rocked Trent back and into his chair. Luckily, everyone was sitting back down, and he doubted they noticed.

"Dearly beloved . . ."

Beloved. Marriage was all about love. He looked at Sarah. What thoughts were running through her head? Was she remembering their own wedding day as he was? Perhaps feeling a bit guilty about taking vows that neither of them had intended to keep?

Melody and Ryan turned to face one another, hands clasped. As Ryan gazed into Melody's eyes and repeated the solemn vow, Trent squirmed uncomfortably in his seat. These were the same words he and Sarah had used, but suddenly they took on a new meaning.

". . . till death do us part."

He looked at Sarah. What would she say if he told her he wanted their marriage to last that long? The expression in her eyes spoke volumes. Not a word had been spoken but there was an understanding between them.

Until a fat raindrop plopped onto his cheek and rolled down and off his chin. She giggled.

"Looks like rain." He wiped his face dry, only to have two more raindrops replace the first.

"Sunshine mixed with rain means a marriage that lasts forever." She sat back and smiled, as the raindrops dropped faster and heavier.

"I now pronounce you husband and wife. Kiss your bride, and let's head for the tent."

The bride and groom didn't stroll down the aisle arm in arm. They ran. The clouds covered the last ray of sunshine, and the rain poured down, saturating the wedding guests. The women scattered, holding beaded purses over their heads in a vain attempt to keep a patch of hair on top of their heads dry.

He grabbed Sarah's hand and prepared to run only to be brought to a jerking halt by the deadweight on the other end of his arm. He looked over his shoulder.

"This is wonderful." She stood with her face tilted to the sky, soaking in the rain.

Her hair fell around her shoulders in soggy ringlets, her makeup was smudged, and she was the most beautiful sight Trent had ever seen. The sheer joy in life as she let the rain sluice over her face hit his chest with the force of a bulldozer.

"Do you remember our wedding, Trent?" She turned to him. He moved a step closer.

"Vaguely."

"It's fuzzy to me, too." She stepped into his embrace and lifted her arms to his shoulders. "Funny, but the only part I remember clearly is this."

She stood on tiptoe, and brushed her lips against his. He pulled her closer, groaning low in his throat. The emotions and passion of their wedding day hit him with twice the force he'd felt then, until he thought he might drown under the swirling emotions. If the downpour didn't drown him first.

He pulled back. His heart ached a little as Sarah stepped out of his arms, her lips twisting in that funny little smile that signaled her disappointment followed by a long sweep of her lashes. He'd better distance himself fast, or he was going to lose what small restraint he had left.

"Let's go toast the happy couple," Sarah suggested.

Here's to forever. He followed behind her wondering, if he meant the toast for Melody and Ryan or for himself.

Chapter Eighteen

One month, six days, five hours—that was how much time Sarah had left until the appeal went before court. The amount of time she had left as Trent's wife and Caitlin and Kyle's mother.

"Can you draw a circle, sweetie?" She sat at the kitchen table with Caitlin and Kyle, as they scribbled on some blank paper.

Kyle drew a crazy, too-big-for-the-page circle.

"Very good." She clapped. She didn't care if it was lopsided. It was a circle, both ends connected. "You're so bright. I'm going to hang this up where Uncle Trent can see it."

She couldn't lose these children. Didn't Trent understand? He should; he'd almost lost them to Nathan Winters. Didn't he understand that the thought of living her days without the twins' bright smiles was like the thought of living without the sun or the salty breeze from the Pacific?

She hugged Caitlin and kissed the top of her sweet-smelling head. "I love you guys so much."

Every day she would tell them how terrific they were and how much she loved them for as long as she was allowed to. If nothing else, she would never regret this time she'd spent. Each moment was precious, and each smile a memory to be stored.

"Picture time." She grabbed the camera she kept nearby these days and snapped a shot of the twins. She planned to have some concrete images to see her through the long lonely days after the marriage ended.

She'd even managed to snap a few shots of Trent. Some with the twins, some when he wasn't aware she was photographing him. The candid shots were her favorite. One of Caitlin and Trent asleep in his recliner on a lazy Sunday afternoon.

The only problem with pictures was that they weren't warm. You couldn't hold them close. But if they were all she was to have, then she'd learn to live with that.

"Love, 'Arah." Kyle patted her hand.

She smiled, her heart melting again and expanding with even more love for this tiny child she'd come to know as well as the one that had grown beneath her breast.

"I love you, too, you sweet child." *And your uncle.* Twice Sarah had said she'd loved Trent. The day they'd returned from their wedding in Vegas and in the courtroom. He hadn't responded either time, so she could only assume he didn't feel the same way.

She sighed. If only there were some way to make him love her, but life and especially love didn't work that way. You couldn't force someone to care about you. It just happened with an unexplainable force.

Love was like the imprint of an angel's touch. It couldn't be seen, but you knew when it was there. It was like a million tiny grains of sand: impossible to pinpoint the source of each grain and each one necessary to make up an entire beach.

If you couldn't define it, how could you seek it? She knew you couldn't. It either was or it wasn't. Only God had control over the emotion. But, even though her love wasn't returned, Sarah was glad she'd been given the gift of loving another.

She now realized she'd never truly loved Paul. She'd loved the idea of having someone. Of knowing someone for years and marrying him and having a child together. When she'd allowed Paul to talk her into giving up her virginity, she'd been needy, wanting someone of her own to love.

Young and foolish, she'd confused sex and love. The result had been an unplanned pregnancy. If she hadn't gotten pregnant, she might never have agreed to marry Paul in the first place.

Then again, she might have. She'd been a different person then. But life made her into the woman she was, and she knew that Paul was a chapter in the book of her past. She'd turned that page long ago and had no desire to reread it.

"Let's clean up this mess, kids. Uncle Ryan is coming to get you."

"Song?" Caitlin asked.

She laughed. The children called Melody "song." Her real name was too difficult for them to say, and Ryan had teasingly taught them to call her Auntie Song.

"Yes, Melody is coming with him. Let's hurry. I have to get ready. Your uncle wanted to discuss something with me over dinner."

He had sounded so serious, Sarah wondered if he wanted to ask for a divorce already. But he couldn't, the appeal wasn't over yet. He had to stay married to her at least for a while longer. At any rate, Sarah was going to make sure she looked her best; she hoped Trent would be impressed.

The red dress outlined every curve in Sarah's body, and the spaghetti straps showed off her shoulders and neckline. He hoped he could keep his hands off her long enough to talk.

What he really wanted to do was drive to the nearest

hotel and rent a room. He needed to get a grip. He wasn't some randy teenager, and Sarah wasn't the prom queen. This was his wife, even if it was in name only, and now he was a father.

"What did you want to talk about?" Sarah asked as he helped her into the car.

He groaned as the dress slid up her legs to reveal more of her thighs.

"We'll talk over dinner." He slammed the passenger door and walked around to the driver's side.

Taking a deep breath and hoping it lasted for a while, he slid into the car. Lord knew once he got another look at those long legs, he wouldn't be taking another breath for a while.

"How are Ryan and Melody holding up to married life?"

"So happy it's disgusting. They can't keep their hands off one another."

He knew the feeling. The only thing he wanted at the moment was to have his hands all over Sarah. Unfortunately, he needed them on the steering wheel, if he wanted to drive.

"They offered to keep the kids overnight, Trent. Said something about practice."

He wasn't sure he wanted the twins getting too used to having another aunt and uncle in their lives. At least not until he and Sarah had come to some sort of understanding. It wouldn't be fair to them should he and Sarah split up. They would lose Sarah and two more people they loved.

"We'll see, okay?"

She shrugged. "Whatever you want."

They drove the rest of the way to the restaurant in silence. He wondered what he'd said that had ticked Sarah off. It was obvious she was angry. Her entire body was twisted away from him as she stared out the passenger window.

Was she angry because he hadn't agreed to the twins' going with Ryan and Melody? She didn't wait for him to open her door but released the handle herself and stood waiting for him to join her. Her lips were turned down slightly at the corners.

"Something wrong, Sarah?"

She opened her mouth as if to say something, then her lips thinned into a straight line, and she shook her head. "Nothing. Let's just enjoy our evening."

"Kinda hard, when you're as prickly as a blowfish."

"Me? You're the one who tenses up when I mention anything that even resembles us acting like a family."

"That's what I want to talk to you about tonight," Trent admitted.

Sarah's body stiffened, and she crossed her arms over her stomach. He frowned. He'd hoped she'd keep an open mind and listen to what he had to say. Maybe brainstorm the pros and cons with him.

"Let's have a drink before we order."

"Good idea. Make mine a double," Sarah said.

"Why don't you have a club soda? I don't want to be accused of getting you drunk. This decision has to be made with a clear head. In fact, I'm having club soda too."

She snorted, but didn't argue.

The lounge was crowded, but he managed to find a corner with two chairs and a low-slung table. The conversation around them was loud enough that he had to lean close to be heard. She smelled of roses and some exotic musky scent that was all her own.

"I'll go get our drinks and be right back."

She nodded. He escaped before he followed through on

his desire to plant a kiss behind her ear and trail it down her throat.

Their relationship had to be approached in a logical manner. There was no other reason for her to agree to his proposal. It had to be kept on a business footing, or it would never work. She would never agree to it.

He ordered their drinks and took a gulp of his soda to calm his nerves. He handed Sarah her club soda. The lounge wasn't the place to discuss his idea. It was noisy, and he didn't want to compete with fifteen other conversations to be heard.

It was only a few minutes before their table was called, and they made their way to a secluded corner table of the dimly lit restaurant. Here the conversation was muted, and soft instrumental music filtered through the speaker system and drowned out what the other tables were saying.

She waited until they'd ordered, then turned to Trent.

"Okay, you need to tell me now. I'm dying of nerves and curiosity."

He chuckled. "Patience is not one of your virtues."

She shrugged. "I'm aware of that. Now tell me."

"I have a proposition for you."

"Doesn't surprise me. This dress has that effect." Sarah's smile was feline.

He felt the heat that rushed into his face. *God, what is she trying to do to me?*

"Why, Trent, I do believe you're blushing."

"Not exactly that type of proposition."

Sarah's smile faded. "I see. Okay, I'm listening."

Why did she look so disappointed? Had she wanted it to be that type of proposition? He'd be more than happy to oblige her if that was the case. But first, they had a few things to discuss.

"I've been thinking about your offer to stay on as the kids' nanny."

Now he had her attention. She leaned forward slightly, and her eyes sparkled with interest. "And?"

"And, I don't think it would work."

"Oh." She swallowed.

"Sarah, they see you as their mother. They're used to having you there every day. To suddenly become their nanny from nine to five or whatever actual hours it would be, would be like ripping you away from them."

"That's why I should be their nanny. It isn't fair to remove me from their life completely. It isn't fair to remove them from mine." Blue eyes pleaded with him to understand.

He did understand. More than she knew. "No. It just won't work."

"Will I get to see them at all?" Sarah whispered.

"That's what I wanted to talk to you about. I had an idea, but I wasn't sure how you'd feel about it."

"If it means I can be in their lives, even in some small way, I'm willing to consider it."

God, was this what he had reduced her to? Himself to? He was forced to use his children to keep her in his life? But he knew what he was about to propose was the best solution for all of them. Anything less would be unacceptable after living together as a family.

"Stay married to me, Sarah." There, he'd said it. He leaned back, waiting for her reaction. He didn't have to wait long.

"What?"

"Anything else would be difficult on the kids."

"What about you, Trent? I thought you didn't want a wife."

"I didn't. But, I want what's best for Caitlin and Kyle. And you're what's best for them right now." *Liar. She's what's best for you, and you know it.*

"If I agree, how long will this be for?" Sarah's hair fell over her shoulders in shimmering waves.

He wanted to bury his hands in it and pull her in close for his kisses.

"Indefinitely."

"What exactly does that mean, Trent? Does it mean until you get tired of having me around? Until one of us finds someone else to love? Or forever?"

He hadn't even considered the possibility that Sarah might fall in love with somebody else. The thought made his nerve endings sing with ferocious energy. She was his. But she wasn't, that was the problem. It was more like she was on loan. A temporary wife.

"I can't answer that, Sarah. I can only say that if you should want out, I would let you out."

She folded her hands together and stared at them a moment. When she raised her blue gaze to his, they were filled with such determination, he almost flinched.

"I will never want out."

Did she mean she didn't want to give up the twins ever? He could understand that, but still she would have that option should she ever choose to use it.

"Was that a yes?" he asked.

"One condition."

Was there always a condition with this woman? First she'd made a request when she'd asked him to marry her. Now, when he asked her to stay married, she had another. Still, if it meant keeping her in their lives, he would agree to anything.

"Name it," Trent said.

"This will be a real marriage, and we will share a bed."

Chapter Nineteen

She watched as Trent's expression went from resigned to absolute shock. Was the thought of sharing her bed that outrageous? If they were going to stay married "indefinitely," she planned to use this extra time convincing Trent Kasey that he could not live without her as his wife. That meant having a real marriage.

When he finally spoke, his voice was a husky purr that washed over her like tiny drops of bubbling champagne. "That condition will be my pleasure."

She swallowed. She'd stepped over the threshold and locked the door behind her. There was no turning back. She only hoped her plan didn't backfire.

"Then we have a deal, Mr. Kasey."

"Later, we shall seal it with a kiss, Mrs. Kasey."

She barely tasted her meal. Her mind was focused on what would happen between them when they returned home. The moment she'd wanted since they'd married was within her reach, and now she was filled with apprehension.

Paul was the only man she'd ever been with. What if she disappointed Trent the way she had Paul? When he'd walked out on her, Paul had made a point to inform her of how frigid she was. That was why he would never marry her, he said. There was no way he was going to marry an Ice Queen *and* be childless.

The silence on the ride home was thick enough to equal a heavy, morning fog. He reached over and took her hand in his.

"Are you nervous, Sarah?" He lifted her hand and placed

a kiss in the palm, closing her fingers over the kiss.

"A little."

"Don't be."

She sighed. It was always best to be honest. She needed to tell him that he might be disappointed and give him a way out of the situation. It was only fair.

"Trent, if you find me—" She bit her lip.

"I find you beautiful."

"No, if you find me—well—frigid, I'll understand if you don't want to follow through."

He pulled the car off the road and put it in park. He turned to her.

"Who said you were frigid?" He held up his palms. "Don't tell me, let me guess. Paul."

"Yes."

"Sarah, no way are you frigid."

He lifted his hand to her neck and rubbed a circle over her throat with his thumb. She shuddered and moved closer.

"That is not the reaction of a frigid woman. Besides, didn't you know that is something small, insecure men tell women to cover their own shortcomings?"

Why hadn't she met him instead of Paul? He was so wonderful. If only he loved her, he'd be perfect. She wanted him with every fiber of her being and realized that he was right. Her reaction to him was not that of a frigid woman. Suddenly she couldn't wait to experience the sensations she knew were waiting for her in his arms.

"Let's go home." Her voice sounded husky to her own ears.

"I say we take Ryan and Melody up on their baby-sitting offer."

"I think you have wonderful ideas, Mr. Kasey."

Sarah's ex-fiancé had called her frigid. Trent couldn't imagine a description further from the truth. They'd come together with enough heat to set the redwoods ablaze.

"Ryan and Melody should be here with the twins anytime." She slid her arms around his waist and laid her cheek against his back. "What are you cooking?"

It felt right. And that was exactly how it shouldn't feel. He pulled away, using the excuse to grab the saltshaker.

"Omelets. I hope you like onion in yours."

She shrugged and hugged her arms tightly against her chest. She must have noticed his withdrawal from her embrace. He stiffened his resolve. He couldn't allow himself to lower the protective wall guarding his heart.

It wasn't fair to Sarah, he knew, but there was still the intense fear that any emotion would be ripped away in the shreds of tragedy. He glanced at his watch, realizing that Ryan was running late.

"If our marriage is . . ." Sarah paused for long breathless moments, cleared her throat, and continued. "If it's 'indefinite,' should I arrange to have my things moved over here?"

He rubbed his hand over his neck. That seemed so permanent. But wasn't that what he'd asked out of her? *Stay married to me, Sarah.*

"Let's take it slowly, okay?"

He turned quickly, shutting out the bright tears in her eyes that shimmered like diamonds threatening to fall. Where was Ryan? He didn't even know if the man was a good driver. What if . . . Trent swallowed the thought.

The twins had to be okay. They were all he had left in this world. Out of the corner of his eye, he saw Sarah leave the kitchen, her shoulders hunched slightly. No. It wasn't smart to care too much. It only led to heartache. His heart cried out for him to go after Sarah, but another, darker part of him couldn't forgive her at that moment. What if he lost Caitlin and Kyle? What if he lost Sarah? What if he lost them all? Fear clutched at him and refused to let go.

The scent of moist earth and strong, deep roots rose to greet Sarah with their welcoming, familiar scent. She jammed the tiny, gardening shovel around the base of a particularly stubborn weed. It refused to budge.

"Dumb weeds." She swiped at a loose tear with her free hand.

She'd disappointed Trent in the bedroom. That much was obvious from his cool reception this morning. Paul had been right. Only she hadn't felt frigid last night. She'd felt as though the deep belly of a volcano bubbled and stewed within her, waiting for release. A release he had given her.

"Come loose." She slung the shovel down and yanked at the weed with all her strength.

"What did that poor plant ever do to you?" Ryan stood, feet slightly sprawled, looking down at her.

"It's stubborn."

"So are you. Maybe you can find common ground." Ryan held a hand down to her.

She took it and allowed him to pull her up. He looked into her face for a full minute.

"That plant upset you. Want me to kick its butt?"

She sniffed. "Nah. I'm going to zap it with some weed killer."

"I take it things didn't go too well with Trent either?"

She glanced toward the house and shrugged. She felt like a visitor in Trent's home. Which she supposed, she really was. He'd asked her to stay, but for how long? He didn't even want her to move her belongings. She'd escaped to a place where she could work out her frustrations and feel welcome—her garden.

"I can't figure out how men's minds work." She placed her hands on her hips and glared.

Ryan patted her cheek. "That's okay, Sis. We don't understand women either. I figure that puts us on equal footing."

"Were the twins good for you?"

"You're kidding, right?" Ryan groaned. "All I can say is that I prayed Melody is only having one at a time."

She laughed. "You bad man."

"I'm kidding. Actually, they were a lot of fun."

"They are busy."

Ryan held out his crooked arm. "Back to the mansion, m'lady?"

"The dungeon you mean." She took his arm and turned toward the house with a determined stride. She had two children to raise. Their uncle might not be interested in a real family, but she was, and she was going to do everything in her power to see that they had all the love they needed.

Chapter Twenty

"Your brother was late." He hugged Caitlin in one arm and Kyle in the other.

"Fifteen minutes."

He glared at her and pressed a kiss to the top of each silky dark head. His hand fisted into Caitlin's jacket, refusing to let go. How was he supposed to survive if anything happened to them? Why couldn't Sarah understand the intense clawing panic that had wedged itself into his mouth like something sour? Fifteen minutes seemed like a lifetime.

"You were worried." Sarah's voice was as soothing as the gentle brush of silk. "Did you think Ryan had an accident?"

He couldn't answer her. The pain of the thought paralyzed him. She stood in the middle of the living room, looking nervous and uncomfortable. She shifted from foot to foot and hugged her arms to herself.

"It's okay to love, Trent. People don't always die." There was a strange catch in her voice, and her eyes had taken on an indescribable light.

She walked from the room, and Trent wanted to kick himself. Did she know? Was it obvious that he refused to let himself love her or anyone? He didn't know, but the tension between them was building. Sooner or later someone or something was going to have to give, or they would be crushed under the weight.

"Come on, Night. Let's go to the beach." She commanded Nightfire to heel, and the dog fell into place at her side.

"Good doggie," Kyle crooned.

She laughed. He picked up new words every day.

"Let's go to the beach, kids."

"Yeah!" Caitlin jumped up and down and clapped her hands.

When they reached the edge of the beach, they kicked off their shoes and let the warm sand squish between their toes. She released Night from his leash, and the dog ran in circles, barking happily at seagulls.

"Night, come." She blew on her metal whistle.

The dog stopped in front of her and sat. After working with him for over a year, he finally seemed to catch on to her training methods.

"My dog wants to sleep inside." Sarah's foot tapped as she stood in the doorway to Trent's office.

He pulled the roll top on his desk closed and swiveled his chair to face her. Every muscle in her body screamed irritation. Her arms were crossed tightly, and annoyance etched tiny lines around her mouth.

He suspected this was about more than her dog.

"That dog is lethal."

"He's actually very well trained."

He chuckled, covered it with a cough, and earned another glare from Sarah. Okay, compared to Princess, Night was a saint.

"As long as an animal feels loved and *wanted,* it can learn. Just like a person."

He rubbed his hand over the back of his neck. A dog in his house. It seemed as though Sarah had taken over every corner of his life. There wasn't a spot in this house where he could escape and not find traces of her. It was the scent of her perfume in the bedroom, the memory of her spooned against him while they slept, the sound of her laughter as she played with the children.

"Sarah, is this about the dog or about us?" He didn't really think she was this aggravated over her dog. It went deeper.

"Both."

She was honest. He liked that trait. He grinned.

"Move the dog inside tonight. Just make sure he understands he relieves himself outside and no chewing."

"Not a problem." She gave him a sloppy military salute and bounded out of the room.

He shook his head. What had he just done? His life was quickly slipping out of his control, and Trent wasn't quite sure how to get it back.

"Night! Noooo." She rescued the half-eaten brown dress shoe from the dog's mouth and collapsed onto the living room floor. "Oh, Night. You can't do this. You've never done this before? Why pick now of all times?"

How was she supposed to tell Trent his brand-new shoes sported tooth marks and a ripped side? Especially when he had to be in court tomorrow afternoon for the hearing. Did she have time to replace the shoes without Trent noticing? She glanced at the gaudy clock on the living room wall. She grimaced. That thing had to go. It had bachelor stamped all over it. A giant piece of wood from some sort of tree, varnished to a high gloss.

Just as the minute hand slid up to mark noon, the phone rang. She jumped, her heart in her throat. The heavy, ash taste of dread filled her mouth, and she picked the phone up with a shaky hand.

"Sarah?" Ryan's voice cracked on the last syllable of her name.

"What's wrong, Ryan?"

"Melody—" He took a deep shuddering breath. "She's lost the baby. Can you come? Please."

She squeezed her eyes tightly shut, pushed aside pain resurfacing and breaking through the wall she'd built like water finding a stress point in a dam.

"We're in Soul's Harbor General. Maternity ward."

"I'm there." She hung up the phone and stared unseeingly at the twins. Okay, how was she supposed to rush to her brother's side when she had two small children to care for?

Making a sudden decision, she jabbed in the phone number she knew as well as her own name. "Mom? I need your help."

A long pause and a hurt sniff. "You can't make it to Sunday dinners, but you want my help?"

She grimaced. Her parents liked Trent and the twins a little too well. She didn't want her mother to get her hopes up about having Caitlin and Kyle as grandchildren. It would save a lot of heartache if the marriage didn't last. Naturally, her mother saw it as a personal insult.

"I'm sorry, Mom. It's a long story. Look, Melody lost the baby, and I want to be there for her. I know what she's going through. Please, Mom. There isn't anyone else to watch the kids."

"She lost the baby!" her mother cried. "This can't be happening again—"

"Mom. Please. Just get here as quickly as you can."

"Oh, all right."

She paced the room nervously until her mother arrived, kissed the woman's powdered cheek, grabbed her handbag, and started for the door.

Caitlin pitched herself at Sarah's legs, clinging with the

strength of an army. She looked down in time to see two huge tears roll down the little girl's face.

"Mama."

A band tightened around Sarah's chest just as it always did when the children slipped and called her Mama. She reached down and brushed the tears away, then knelt to Caitlin's level.

"Caitlin. I will be back, and Daddy will be home soon. But there is an emergency, and Sarah needs to go."

Caitlin tilted her head to the side, looked at Sarah with two liquid brown eyes, and wailed. "No go!"

"Just go, Sarah. She'll be fine."

Kyle stuck his thumb in his mouth and looked at her as though he would never see her again.

"Oh, maybe I should just—"

"Go! For goodness sake, Sarah. I had four children. They all do this, and if you let them get by with it, they'll be worse next time. I guarantee you they'll be fine five minutes after you leave."

Her mother was right, but that didn't make it any easier to drop a light kiss on each child's head and walk out the door, their wails following her like a siren's song.

She sat in the Explorer for a minute, her knuckles clutched tightly around the steering wheel, wanting to cry herself.

"They'll be fine." With one last look toward the house, she pulled out of the driveway.

The first thing that struck Sarah was the smell and sound of the maternity ward. The milky white smell of baby powder, and the gently cooing babies. A soft gasp escaped her, and she felt the blood drain from her face.

A passing nurse laid a gentle hand on her arm. "Are you okay?"

She nodded. "I-I'm looking for Melody Goldwyne's room."

"Room 305." The nurse nodded toward the far end of the hall.

"T-thank you," Sarah said around chattering teeth.

If she felt this flash of loneliness for a child she'd never hold in her arms, what must Melody be feeling? Melody, whose pain was fresh and raw. Why in the world hadn't they moved her from the maternity ward?

Melody lay on the narrow cot in a drab, mud-colored room. Her hand lay over her abdomen in a tightly clenched fist, and she stared toward the wall of windows on the far side of the room.

A fresh agony seared Sarah's heart. The child had been her niece or nephew. She'd been so busy feeling envious that yet another woman would have a child when she herself couldn't, that she'd failed to really extend friendship to her new sister-in-law. Her attempts had been halfhearted.

"Sis." Ryan rose to greet her, his face looking haggard and half-shaven.

"For God's sake, Ryan, go get something to eat or something."

"I didn't want to leave Melody." He frowned.

"I'll sit with her." She pulled a chair around the bed and set it in front of Melody's nose. Hard to ignore someone when they were in your face.

"Melody, sweetheart, can I get you something to eat?" Ryan brushed his hand against Melody's smooth forehead.

She shook her head no but didn't look at him.

"I won't be gone long."

"Take your time, Ryan. I'll take good care of her."

He nodded but looked back three times on his way out the door. As it swished softly closed behind him, Melody breathed a sigh of relief.

"Thank you. If he'd said one more thing, I would have screamed."

"Let me guess." She tapped her forefinger against her lips. "We can try to have another baby. There was probably something wrong with this one. And—my favorite—it was God's will."

Melody's eyes filled with tears, and a shadow passed over her heart.

"I didn't mean to make you cry, Melody."

The young woman grabbed a handful of nearby tissues and dabbed at her red, swollen eyes. "It's not your fault, Sarah. I can't seem to stop."

"I guess what I was trying to let you know was that I have been through this."

"Ryan told me. I'm so glad you came." Melody twisted the tissues into a tight rope, and then back the other way. "Sarah, does it ever get easier?"

Did it? She wasn't so sure about that, but it did change. She didn't want to lie to Melody, but she didn't want to upset her either.

"It lessens some. There will always be moments when it's more difficult, but I suspect having another child helps a little. If I'd been able to—" Her throat closed off, and she had to blink to stop the tears threatening.

Melody reached out and laid her hand on Sarah's. "It's okay, Sarah."

"Look at me." Sarah grabbed a few of the tissues out of the box. "I'm here to make you feel b-better, and I'm bl-blubbering all over the place."

"You are helping, Sarah." Melody clasped her hand tightly.

"I always wanted a sister, Melody."

"Me too." Melody's smile was shy and hopeful.

"I'd like it very much if we could be close," Sarah said.

"If I'm married to Ryan long enough." Melody shrugged, unhappiness tugging the corners of her lips down.

"What nonsense. Ryan loves you."

"No. He married me because of the baby."

"Melody." Did she really believe that? "Ryan loves you. I know my brother."

"You really think so?"

"I know so."

A look of such relief and joy washed over Melody's features that Sarah would beat the living tar out of Ryan if he didn't come back in here and let this poor woman know how much she was loved. It was no fun believing your husband didn't love you.

She frowned. If Melody believed Ryan didn't care, perhaps she'd misjudged Trent, too? What if he was able to love her more than she suspected? Was she giving up too soon?

"Don't give up, Sarah." Melody's words echoed Sarah's thoughts so closely Sarah gave a startled jump.

"Beg pardon?"

"On Trent. Don't give up. He can learn to love. Just look at how much he loves those children."

Was Melody right? Was it somehow possible to break through that huge ice wall of Trent's heart and find love? Or at least fondness. She'd settle for that. Any feeling from him would have to be enough.

Chapter Twenty-One

"Sarah. What happened to my shoes?" Trent's voice thundered through the house, shaking the sound waves and scattering them into chaos.

Uh-oh. Sarah grabbed Night and shoved him out the back door the second before Trent stomped into the kitchen. He held one tattered brown shoe in his hand. His other hand was on his hip. He looked big and furious and utterly gorgeous.

She grinned.

"This isn't funny, Sarah." If a look could define "mean," this was it.

"Sorry, Trent." Sarah tried not to smile. "I'll buy you a new pair."

"Before this afternoon?"

"Yes." She wiped her hands on her jeans. She'd been planning to bake cookies for the twins, but it could wait. The dough would keep in the refrigerator. She'd completely forgotten the shoes. "I'll go now."

"Wait." He crossed his arms. "What about the twins?"

"Can't you watch them? They are yours, too."

"I had planned to catch up on paperwork."

And you're only here because he needs a nanny, Sarah reflected with bitterness. "Fine. I'll take them with me."

She slammed the bowl of cookie dough onto the second shelf of the fridge and shut the door with more force than was necessary. It sprang back open, so Sarah gave it a sharp kick for good measure.

"Sarah?"

"What?" She knew her voice was sharp, but she was tired of playing the sweet-nice Sarah. The one who put up with being treated like a fixture.

Her first indication that he'd moved closer was the citrus tang of lime in the air. He ran one hand down her arm.

"I'm sorry. Just nervous about the hearing, I guess."

Sarah relaxed. *Okay, so maybe being a fixture isn't so bad when he touches me like that.*

"I meant to replace the shoes, but with Melody . . ." She trailed off.

"I know. It's okay. I'll go replace the shoes. You stay here and do what you do best."

Silence filled the room as he turned toward the doorway. What did he mean by that?

"What do I do best, Trent?"

He turned, the half-confused look on his face clearing slightly.

"Make our house a home."

And then he was gone, leaving Sarah stunned, and a little hopeful.

He had lost count of the prayers he'd sent heavenward. Did praying hard make a difference? He didn't know, but he was going to do his best. There was little else left for him to do. He'd married. He'd cut back his hours at work.

"It'll work out." Sarah squeezed his hand a little too tightly, and Trent winced.

Her reassuring squeeze had a tinge of desperation in it. In the four months since they'd met her on the beach, she had grown to love the twins, that was obvious from her interaction with them. To lose Caitlin and Kyle would be almost as devastating to her as it would be to him.

"That bastard looks like the perfect doting father."

Nathan Winters leaned back in his chair and smirked at them, his expression in direct contrast with the conservative suit and hair parted to one side.

"He would probably fool me," Sarah admitted.

"Nathan Winters is not raising my children."

"Your sister's children, you mean."

He frowned. When had he started to think of Caitlin and Kyle as his? Of course they had ties that wouldn't have existed if they were his. If they were his, he wouldn't be sitting in this courtroom with the core of his future in the hands of some apathetic judge.

"All rise."

The judge entered the room with a swish of robes, a pound of the gavel, and an order for them to be seated. Trent took a deep breath and held it, thankful for Sarah's family supporting him just one row back.

"Let's get this over quickly. These children have been in limbo too long as it is." The judge glared at Trent.

Why not glare at Nathan Winters? He was the one appealing the original decision. His brow beaded with an icy sweat. If he lost Caitlin and Kyle . . .

"I'm well aware that Mr. Kasey probably married to expedite the custody of the children to his name." The judge glared at Sarah as if she were a particularly offensive bug who'd dared to cross in front of his shoe.

Every protective instinct in Trent reared to life. Sarah had done nothing wrong. If loving two children and putting their well-being above your own desires was wrong, then he didn't care much for the judicial system. He raised his arm and placed it around Sarah's shoulders, lending her the strength of his own body while shielding her partially from the menace that was Nathan Winters.

"And Mr. Winters, is there anything else you'd like to add?"

"My client feels that the children's money may not be in the best hands, Your Honor." The lawyer sniffed and nodded toward Trent.

"That low-down—"

"Hush, darling." She reached her hand up and twined her fingers with his.

The touch of her hand sent heat spiraling up his arm. He forced himself to calm down. An outburst certainly wouldn't help their case any.

The judge tapped his forefinger against his lips, obviously in deep thought. Trent's stomach clenched. Midnight black fright swept through him. Was this how Sarah felt at the thought of a life without children? This empty barren feeling . . . as though to take one more breath would hurt more than to simply stop breathing. How had she borne it? How did one survive losing a child?

He realized that Sarah was much stronger than he gave her credit for, and his admiration of her increased another notch. This woman never failed to amaze him. Each time he felt as though he was beginning to know her, something happened to make him realize he had barely scratched the surface.

"It is irregular to award the same person custody and control over the estate. So, here is my proposal." The judge smiled a twisted, catlike smile.

Ice jabbed through Trent's veins, and Sarah's hand squeezed his so hard it started to cut off the circulation. He pulled her closer, needing her warmth to chase away the chill.

"Mr. Winters, you shall be awarded custody of the children."

Sarah sucked in her breath in a painful wail. "Nooo."

Trent felt as though someone had reached into his chest and ripped his heart out. Would he even be given visitation?

All he could think was how miserable Caitlin and Kyle would be. Why hadn't he signed a check when Nathan had offered to drop the custody battle in exchange for the money? He could make more money; he couldn't replace those two children. Nor could he make their lives okay once Nathan Winters had them in his evil grasp. Everything in the room faded away. The judge's voice drifted into nonsensical syllables.

"No . . . no . . . no." She whispered a chant of denial.

"However, Mr. Kasey shall remain in control of any equities associated with the estate. You will be solely responsible for the children's care, as Mr. Kasey has been these past months. Miss Kasey was not a wealthy woman, and there will be no financial support for the care of the children. There is only a life insurance policy, which Miss Kasey has requested be put aside for their college."

Silence echoed through the courtroom. Trent swallowed. He didn't want to be in control of the money. He wanted the children. He opened his mouth to speak, but Nathan Winters's voice cut across the interior of the chamber in a loud boom like thunder.

"That is unacceptable."

Sarah choked. He patted her on the back, feeling her misery as though it rolled off her in waves.

"I would think you'd be thrilled the children are going to be with you. I can see from the home study that you are financially solvent, so their upkeep should be no problem. It is the opinion of this court that if your motives are that of a loving, caring parent, your first concern will be to secure the children into your custody."

"I think what my client means to say is that he would prefer to be in charge of the estate so that he can see that it stays in the right hands."

He leaned back in his chair. He would appeal this. No way was Winters raising Caitlin and Kyle. He'd take it to the Supreme Court if he could, if he had to. He'd fight until there wasn't breath in his body.

"We'll appeal, Sarah," he whispered against her temple.

Her body trembled but she'd grown suddenly alert. "Shh. Just listen."

The judge leaned forward and stared at Nathan Winters with the clear, judicious eyes of wisdom. "I'm well aware of whose hands Mr. Winters wants the money in. I have not sat on this bench for twenty years without coming to know something about human nature and greed. My decision stands."

The judge paused. She chewed her lower lip. He clenched his fists. Aruba? Switzerland? Canada? Where could they go if they weren't allowed to appeal? Could he bring himself to break the law and run away with the children? How could he turn them over to Winters knowing what a greedy bastard the man was?

Lord help him. He didn't know what to do.

"Unless . . ." The judge stared at Winters. "You prefer to drop the appeal?"

Winters cursed, conferred with his lawyer.

"Brilliant," Sarah said, and crossed her arms. A slight smile tilted the corners of her mouth.

He frowned. He'd been distracted by the implications of what the judge had said and somehow had stopped listening to the words. He wasn't exactly sure what was going on, but apparently Sarah had figured it out. "My client will drop the appeal and all future claims to the children."

"No visitation?"

"No."

"Case closed." The judge turned to Trent and Sarah. "Mr. and Mrs. Kasey, take good care of those children."

"We will, Your Honor." She winked at the judge.

Trent's mouth dropped open as the judge winked back.

"What just happened?" He rubbed his hand over his eyes.

His emotions had just Ping-Ponged in a thousand different directions, and he wasn't sure he was capable of thinking at the moment.

"What just happened was that we got the savviest judge in the history of court cases. He is Matlock and Perry Mason rolled into one. Okay, so they weren't judges, but you get the idea." She threw her arms around his neck and kissed him.

It only took Trent's body a second to respond to her touch. *Not good,* he thought. It wasn't smart to feel as close to her as he was feeling at the moment. But the thought was halfhearted.

He gently pulled away, nevertheless. She sighed, as the corners of her mouth turned down.

"Looks like you won, Kasey." Nathan Winters stopped beside their table and growled at them in his gruff, Rough Man Winter voice.

"The only winners were the children."

"I'll be watching the money. You'd better be on the straight and narrow."

He started to stand, but Sarah laid a hand on his arm.

"Mr. Winters, can I show you something?" Sarah asked him.

The man glared at her and crossed his arms. "Make it quick. I'm a busy man."

She opened her purse and pulled out a snapshot of Caitlin and Kyle. He recognized it as a picture she'd taken last week. The children were on either side of Night, each with a chubby, toddler arm wrapped around his big furry

180

neck. They laughed into the camera, and Trent's throat closed with longing as he realized how much they resembled his sister.

"They look like me." Nathan Winters reached out for the picture with a shaking hand.

"They're your children, Mr. Winters. How can you not love them?" Sarah's eyes sparkled with unshed tears.

He could almost feel the depth of her sorrow reaching out to Nathan Winters; it was like invisible fingers stretching out and offering a lifeline.

Winters's face crumpled into fold upon fold of misery.

"I learned years ago that to love only causes heartache. The sooner you learn that, the better off you'll be."

"If you can't love, you're going to die a bitter, lonely old man." Sarah's words could have been aimed at Winters or at Trent. It was hard to tell.

He swallowed. Was that how he'd be if he refused to open his heart to love, to risk again? Would he become the very thing he most hated?

Winters's mouth worked, but he didn't respond. She pressed the picture into his hand.

"Keep it. Someday, when you're able to open your heart, maybe you can find a common ground with your children through that picture."

Without a word, Nathan Winters turned and walked away.

He watched him as though looking into a mirror a few years in the future. My God, was that what he would become? Was Nathan Winters the result of a man refusing to allow himself to love? He refused to become his enemy. But how could he stop it? How could he find the courage to allow his heart to open to love again? To the possibility of loss and pain and despair?

Chapter Twenty-Two

For the third day in a row, Sarah collapsed at the same time as the twins. She never took naps during the day, but she was just so tired.

"Night, behave." The dog laid his head on his paws and whined a bit.

The front door slammed, and Sarah sat up and scooted to the edge of the bed. "Trent?"

He appeared in the bedroom doorway, his shirtsleeves rolled up and showing his muscled forearms. Was everything about the man sexy?

"You're early."

"Thought I'd treat you to Chinese." He held up a heavy paper bag.

The smell of steamed rice and fried wonton wafted across the room. Sarah's stomach rebelled.

"Oh, boy." She held her head in her hands.

"Are you okay?" Trent set the bag down and knelt in front of her.

"I think I have a cold. I'll be fine."

"Why don't you rest? I'll take care of the twins."

"Bless you." She lay back on the bed. She hadn't felt this rotten since her pregnancy.

Sleep had almost taken over when she sat bolt upright in bed.

"Oh, my God." It wasn't possible. Was it?

Sarah's hands shook as she unfolded the white sheet of instructions.

"Here goes a waste of time." There was no way she could be pregnant. Her missed period, queasiness, and exhaustion were just a coincidence.

"Except I'm never late." She looked in the mirror, noticing the pale skin and dark circles. She looked about as good as she felt.

She followed the directions and set the test aside. In about five minutes the results would come back negative, then she could stop fantasizing and get on with her life.

" 'Arah?" Kyle stood in the doorway.

"Sweetie, why are you out of bed? It's nap time." She picked Kyle up and he snuggled himself into her arms, laying his head on her shoulder.

She tucked him in and glanced at the clock. Ten minutes had passed. Rushing to the bathroom, she closed her eyes for a moment before picking up the white test case and staring blankly at the plus sign.

Positive.

"I let it sit too long." She had prepared for this. She had two more tests on hand for retests.

"Here goes nothing again."

Five minutes later a plus sign stared back at her in glaring red clarity.

Ten minutes later, the third test showed positive.

Hope uncurled through Sarah as her hand fell to her belly.

"A baby." She smiled, cherishing the thought. "A miracle." Would Trent think so? How was she ever going to tell him?

Needing some time and space to absorb the fact that she was going to have a baby, Sarah packed the twins and the dog into her Explorer and headed for a local park.

While the twins chased Night, trying to retrieve the Frisbee, Sarah sat on a bench and absorbed the warm rays of fall sunshine.

"A baby." She laid her hand on her still flat abdomen. "You have no idea how wanted you are."

How would Caitlin and Kyle like having a baby brother or sister? How would Trent take the news? She had to tell him, but she might keep the secret to herself for just a little longer. Take some time to savor the marvel of the life growing within her. Try to figure out how to tell him.

A squirrel scampered across Night's line of sight, and the dog cowered back.

"You big chicken." She laughed.

The day had grown dim, late-afternoon shadows sweeping across the grass. She'd have to hurry, or they wouldn't make it home before Trent did.

"Kyle, Caitlin, Night. Time to go."

He pushed back the curtains and stared at the still-empty driveway. Where were they? The clock on the wall showed six o'clock.

She'd seemed distracted this morning when he'd left. He had just assumed she still wasn't feeling well.

"Why didn't she leave a note?" What if there'd been an accident. Pushing the thought away, Trent paced from the window to the kitchen doorway and back again.

"Where is she?"

He pushed his hands through his hair, wishing for a crystal ball he could look into and discover Sarah's whereabouts. She knew how he worried. Why didn't she call?

Ten minutes later the phone rang. Thank, God. He

grabbed the phone from its hook, relief sweeping through him.

"Mr. Kasey?" The soft voice on the other end of the line was the same voice he'd heard the night of his sister's accident. He'd never forget that voice. It was a nurse at Soul's Harbor General.

"Just tell me."

"Your wife has been in an accident."

Trent's mouth went dry, the taste of defeat was like heavy ashes. This couldn't be happening again. It just couldn't. The nurse's voice faded into the background as he tried to comprehend how fate could be so cruel.

"The twins." Was that his voice that sounded so choked?

"Oh, the children are fine, Mr. Kasey. One of the nurses is in the waiting room with them."

Relief flooded through Trent, only to be replaced with heavy dread. Sarah. He dropped the phone into the cradle and rushed for his Camaro.

An image of Sarah dipping a strawberry into champagne and slowly lifting it to her lips flooded his vision. He had to blink several times to clear it, only to have it followed by an image of her leaning over the twins' beds and kissing them on the forehead. He blinked several times, feeling the moisture behind the images.

"Sarah?" Dr. Monroe stood at the foot of her bed.

She blinked back tears. "Tell me the worst. I either wasn't pregnant at all, or I've lost the baby, right?"

Dr. Monroe smiled, his gentle brown eyes crinkling at the corners. "You are most definitely pregnant, and the baby seems to be fine. You'll want to come into my office for a regular prenatal visit though. Until then, I've written you a prescription for vitamins."

185

"The baby is okay?" Sarah whispered, her hand covering the growing life within her.

"Ultrasound came back perfect. You're about ten weeks."

"And you're certain the twins are okay?"

"Not so much as a scratch."

She closed her eyes. "Thank God."

"I had one of our nurses call your husband. He's on his way."

"No." She bit her lip. "I mean, don't tell him about the baby. I want to tell him myself."

"As you wish." The doctor left the room with a swish of his jacket.

She lay back on the pillows. Trent's worst fear was losing the twins. She'd been driving the car when they got in an accident. Whether it was her fault or not, he wasn't going to be pleased.

Kyle and Caitlin lay curled into sleeping balls on the fake leather sofa in the waiting room. Trent wanted to scoop them into his arms and never let them go. He could have lost them so easily.

"Mr. Kasey? The doctor is finished with your wife, if you'd like to go in now." The nurse smiled at the twins. "I'll stay here with them."

Sarah wasn't in intensive care. Surely that was a good sign? He hadn't spoken with the doctor yet; the attending physician had been on rounds. Taking a deep breath, Trent stood and headed for Room 236.

Sarah's honey lashes lay against her face like dark halos of exhaustion. He frowned. Had she looked exhausted this morning, or had the accident etched that weariness onto her face?

Her lashes fluttered and opened.

"Trent. I'm so sorry. The twins are fine."

"Shh."

"It wasn't my fault. The idiot that rear-ended us was drinking."

"It's okay, Sarah. I'm just relieved that everyone is okay."

She seemed to relax. He wanted to pull her into his arms and make sure she was really okay, but a part of him didn't want to get that close. He'd almost lost her today, proving that caring led to heartache. He'd known better than to let himself care this much about anyone. He never wanted to feel that tight panicked feeling again.

"We're all fine."

Then why did it feel like his heart had been ripped out? Half of him wanted to walk away from Sarah and save his heart. The other half wanted to hold on to her forever and hold back the lonely bitterness that threatened. He wasn't sure which half was stronger.

Chapter Twenty-Three

"Sarah, we need to talk," Trent said five days after she came home from the hospital.

Oh, no. Here it comes. He's going to tell me to leave. Well, the accident hadn't been her fault, and if he wanted to cut her out of his life over it, he was going to have a fight on his hands.

"Okay. Let's talk." Sarah nodded, feeling decidedly queasy, a condition the doctor had confirmed was a miracle. Her hand slipped down to gently protect the life growing within her. Avoid stress. Avoid strenuous activity. Take it easy, the doctor had said.

Normally, she loved the scent of Trent's lime aftershave, but as he stepped closer, the scent of burnt dinner biscuits mixed with his citrusy cologne assaulted her already hypersensitive nose. Sarah threw her hand over her mouth, mumbled an excuse me, and rushed for the bathroom.

Just her luck. The man was ready to dump her like an unwanted toy and instead of being tough enough to give him a piece of her mind, she wound up wrapped around a toilet bowl.

Did she care? Nope. Her hand spread across her stomach. She'd suffer any humiliation God threw her way for this baby. Hers. Hers and Trent's. A miracle from God.

Tap. Tap. Tap. "Sarah? Are you okay?"

Trent's voice soothed her more than the cool water she was splashing on her cheeks.

"Yes. I'll be out in a second."

Sarah brushed her teeth, retouched her makeup—might

as well look gorgeous, Trent could eat his heart out—and made her way toward the sound of someone moving around the kitchen.

"I thought we'd be less likely to disturb the twins in here, since they are actually asleep early for a change," Trent explained, as she raised her brows at the cups of coffee.

Trent handed her a mug, leaning down to whisper. "I added a little something to make it a nightcap."

Sarah sniffed at the coffee and realized it had enough Irish in it to put an army to sleep. She set it on the counter. Better pass. Not good for the baby.

He stepped closer.

"Just as I thought. Were you planning on telling me you were pregnant?" Trent's breath stirred the hair at her temple.

"I guess now I don't have to. How did you guess?"

"The mad rush for the bathroom." His hands settled on her hips, and he pulled her in close to him.

"How do you feel about a baby, Trent?" It shouldn't matter. The baby was a miracle whether he wanted it or not. But it did matter. It mattered more than anything else ever had.

"That depends."

A flash of pure irritation shot through her. What would it take to get this man to realize they were *already* a family?

"Depends on what?"

"Are you staying with us, Sarah? Will you remain my wife?"

The shadows in his eyes suddenly cleared, and Sarah saw his deep fear. He was scared she was going to leave him. Why would he be frightened over that? Was he scared that she would take the baby and leave him without anyone to watch over Caitlin and Kyle? But she'd already made it clear that she wanted to remain a part of their lives no matter what. So what exactly was he scared of?

"I'm staying."

"For how long?" Trent's hand trembled a little as he raised it to brush her jaw.

"Indefinitely."

"I was hoping for something a little more specific this time." His warm green eyes reminded her of that first day they'd met, when he'd looked up at her from his not-so-soft landing in the sand.

"I'm open to negotiation."

"How about forever?"

Sarah's breath slammed into her lungs. She forced herself to release it.

"Somewhere along the way I overcame my fear of loving again, Sarah. It may have been that first day when all I could see was miles of leg. Or maybe it was later when you burned pancakes and chased after the twins, or it's possible it was the first time you said you loved me."

"You love me?" When did hope stop holding its breath and begin to live again? Was it with the sudden trembling bloom of a morning glory? Perhaps it was a slower, more gradual process.

"I think I always have. I was just too frightened to admit it. I've lost everyone I've ever loved, Sarah."

"I'm not going anywhere."

He shook his head. "Sometimes people are taken from you, even when they don't want to leave."

She frowned. "You still sound scared."

"There is a part of me that will always worry when you're five minutes late. But I know the secret now. We can't shut down and stop loving because there is a risk involved with the giving of that emotion."

"Smart man."

"To do so would turn me into a bitter man like Nathan Winters. It's better to love for a short time than to avoid it and live with that pain."

"I love you, Trent Kasey." She planted a gentle kiss on his chin.

He smirked. "I know."

"And I love Caitlin and Kyle. This new baby won't change that."

"I know that, too. Sarah, you are the best thing that could have happened to those children."

"They're the best thing that could have happened to me."

"You're all the best thing that could have happened in my life." Trent's voice was husky with emotion.

He moved his hands to cup her still flat belly. A look of wonder passed over his face, and Sarah knew that this baby would be the most loved baby ever to grace the West Coast. She smiled at the twins, love filling her heart. With Caitlin and Kyle leading the way, Sarah wondered what adventures this baby would bring.

About the Author

Lori Soard has a Ph.D. in Journalism and Creative Writing. Thousands of her articles and short stories have been published and several books through small presses. In 1997, she opened wordmuseum.com, a multi-genre site for readers and writers. She's spoken across the country on topics related to cutting edge fiction and hosts a semi-weekly workshop on America Online for writers. She was co-founder and served as the first Chairperson for World Romance Writers and currently sits on the board of Romance Writers of America.

She lives in the Midwest with her husband and two daughters. The family includes a Golden Retriever, Miniature Dachshund, and three cats. The latest addition to the family is a kitten rescued from the local animal shelter. Sassy loves to curl up right on top of Lori's computer while she's trying to write.

Lori loves to hear from her readers. You can contact her at LASoard@aol.com, or write to her at P.O. Box 452, Greenfield, IN 46140. You can also visit her Web site at www.lorisoard.com.